THE TYPE-WRITER GIRL.

THE
TYPE-WRITER GIRL

BY

OLIVE PRATT RAYNER

LONDON
C. ARTHUR PEARSON LIMITED
HENRIETTA STREET W.C.
1897

CONTENTS.

CHAP.   PAGE

    I. —INTRODUCES A LATTER-DAY HEROINE   ...   9

   II. —THE STRUGGLE FOR LIFE   18

   III. —ENVIRONMENT WINS   29

   IV. —THE CHOICE OF A PATRON   41

   V. —VIVE L'ANARCHIE !   47

   VI. —THE INNER BROTHERHOOD   60

   VII. —A MUTINOUS MUTINEER   68

   VIII. —CALLED "OF ACCIDENTS"   83

   IX. —I PLAY CARMEN   95

   X. —SIC ME SERVAVIT APOLLO !   104

   XI. —A SAIL ON THE HORIZON   114

   XII. —A CAVALIER MAKES ADVANCES   131

   XIII. —CONCERNING ROMEO   137

   XIV. —"NOW BARABBAS WAS A PUBLISHER"   ...   145

   XV. —FRESH LIGHT ON ROMEO   155

   XVI. —I TRY LITERATURE   165

   XVII. —A DRAWN BATTLE   176

   XVIII. —AN AUTUMN HOLIDAY   194

   XIX. —"O ROMEO, ROMEO !"   203

   XX. —"WHEREFORE ART THOU ROMEO ?"   ...   223

   XXI. —ENVOY PLENIPOTENTIARY   242

   XXII. —I CLING TO THE RIGGING   253

THE TYPE-WRITER GIRL.

CHAPTER I.

INTRODUCES A LATTER-DAY HEROINE.

I WAS twenty-two, and without employment.

I would not say by this that I was without
occupation. In the world in which we live,
set with daisies and kingfishers and unde-
ciphered faces of men and women, I doubt
I could be at a loss for something to occupy
me. A swallow's back, as he turns in the
sunshine, is so full of meaning. If you dwell
in the country, you need but pin on a hat
and slip out into a meadow, and there, in
some bight of the hedgerow, you shall see
spring buds untwisting, sulphur butterflies
coquetting ; hear nightingales sing as they
sang to Keats, and streamlets make madrigal
as they wimpled for Marlowe. Nay, even
here in London, where life is rarer, how can
I cruise down the Strand without encounter-

ing strange barks—mysterious argosies that
attract and intrigue me ?   That living stream
is so marvellous !   Whence come they, these
shadows, and whither do they go ? — in-
numerable, silent, each wrapped in his own
thought, yet each real to himself as I to my
heart.   To me, they are shooting stars,
phantoms that flash athwart the orbit of my
life one second, and then vanish.   But to
themselves they are the centre of a world
—of *the* world ; and I am but one of the
meteors that dart across their horizon.

I cannot choose but wonder who each is,
and why he is here.   For one after another I
invent a story.   It may not be the true story,
but at least it amuses me.   Every morning I
see them stream in from the Unknown, by the
early trains, and disperse like sparks that
twinkle on the thin soot of the chimney-back
—men with small black bags, bound for
mysterious offices.   What happens in those
offices I have no idea : they may lend money,
or buy shares, or promote Christian knowledge.   I only know I see them come in the
morning and flit again at night, sometimes the
same figures, recognisably identical.   They
rush back, absorbed, to catch the train to the
Unknown, as they rushed up from it earlier.

So, day after day, the tide sets and ebbs; while I stand on the shore of the vast sea of London like a child that watches. And Commissioner Lin guards me.

I have always been grateful to Mr. Samuel Butler for his eccentric theory that a woman wrote the Odyssey. I do not say that I agree with him ; if I did, I am not aware that any critic would attach the least importance to my opinion. But it is a soothing theory for us latter-day women. Without thinking it true, I love to believe it. The Odyssey, you will grant, is the epic of the imagination. It is the epic of mystery. In the Iliad, which is the epic of fact, everything is clear-cut, distinct, commonplace. I do not conceive that a woman could have written the Iliad. Its theme would fail to interest her. That hard handplay of battle counts for nought to our sex. Clang of bronze sword on ringing shield rouses no echo in our heart or brain. It is a masculine poem. How practical it is, how cold, how everyday, how mannish ! Considering its august age, how little it gleams with the glamour of antiquity ! Ulysses in the Iliad is just a shifty politician, an adroit public speaker. Achilles is just a petulant, ill-disciplined young warrior—I hav met him

B 2

in London, fresh home from the Transvaal.
The whole mighty saga is a saga of men's
ideas, so sharp is it in its outlines, so his-
torical, so definite.   But the Odyssey!

Yes, I read in it clearly the fine hand of a
woman.   It has the vagueness, the elusive-
ness, the melting, hazy charm of feminine
craft.   It thrills with mystery ; and woman
is the mystic.   Look at its glorious dimness.
You descry its geography in veiled outline
only, as one beholds the Paps of Jura on a
day of sea-fog through swaying sheets of
white cloud from a fisherman's boat on the
Bay of Oban.   It is a Celtic dreamland.
From morning to night, in that enchanted
poem, on and on we sail, past uncertain isles
or dubious blue headlands, begirt with fantastic forms, and in perils of the sea more
awesome than the real.   Architects have re-
constructed Priam's palace, I believe, from
the description in the Iliad.   That is man's
way of describing.   But who could reconstruct,
from the rapt words of the Odyssey, Circe's
island or the gardens of Alcinous ?   Peering
and prying Schliemann found in the battle-
epic a whole plan of the Troad ; or, at least,
read one into it : fancy even imagining you
could construct a chart of the Mediterranean

to show the homeward maze of the much-
travelled wanderer from Ilion to Ithaca !
The bare idea would indicate a misconception
of the Odyssey.   For those are the seas and
islands that never were ; they live but in the
ghost-geography of poets and women.

As arguments, indeed, the proofs adduced
seem to me preposterous.   It is nonsense to
say that in the Odyssey the chief *rôle* is played
by women.   Do women's books deal exclu-
sively, or even mainly, with their own sex ?
Is not the Titan man, the strong, sardonic,
woman-quelling hero, a recognised commonplace of women's fancy ?   I do not believe an
Ithacan lady wrote the Odyssey *because* of the
relative importance of Penelope and Nausicaa.
Surely even a man might have set Penelope
at her web, or Nausicaa at her tennis.   In
that I see nothing occult or esoterically
feminine.   Men must be aware that every
Circe has the power of turning men into
swine.   They ought to know; they have seen
it done daily.   No, those are not the reasons
that weigh with me.   It is the wonder, the
magic, the purple mystery, of the Odyssey
that tells to my mind in favour of its female
authorship.   And though I know Mr. Samuel
Butler's theory is not true, I thank God I

am woman enough none the less to embrace
it.

But what has all this to do with my story
—the story I am setting out in my own
fashion to tell you? A great deal; and
besides, unless you let me tell it in my own
wayward way, I can never get through with
it. In that respect also I hold myself true
woman. And this is the connection. "If
only we could have lived in those days!"
people say. I answer, "You *are* living in
them." It is not the days, not the places,
not the things that change, but we who
see them otherwise. Consider, the Mediterranean is the same sea to-day as when
the Ithacan lady who wrote the Odyssey
looked out upon its blue zones to behold
it peopled with strange forms and wizard
shadows. For that nameless Sappho, that
prehistoric Charlotte Brontë, that inchoate
Elizabeth Barrett Browning, the Ionian main
swarmed alive with Gorgons and Harpies
as Loch Fyne with herrings. Sirens sang
on every rock to lure the seaman; promontories glowed red at set of sun with the
forges of the Cyclops. You may steam down
the prosaic Adriatic to-day in an Austrian
Lloyd steamer—a fearsome Behemoth, bel-

lowing, snorting, flame-breathing—and identify those charmed shores of Hellenic fancy, as laid down, with soundings, in the Admiralty surveys. But that is your blindness. Scylla and Charybdis are there as of old : 'tis you who turn them into the Straits of Messina. Polyphemus still haunts his seaward cave : 'tis you who transform him into a custom-house officer. Adventures are to the ad-venturous. Go through the world in search of Calypso, and you will surely find her. Be modern, and you will find only Willesden Junction. That may suffice for you. I live in "those days," as all lovers of the mystical have always lived in them.

And I will go forth into the world in search of adventures. They are sure to come to me ; for faith moves mountains. In every age, when the Princess Cleodolind is sent out from the city as a prey for the dragon, some youthful St. George, in celestial armour, rides by in the nick of time, on his snow-white steed, and draws his trusty blade, and fights for her, and rescues her from the loathly thing. Else what were the use of faith and of poetry ? In every age we fashion the story anew in our passing manner, dressing it up in our own clothes, and fitting it to our

particular modes and morals. But 'tis the
same to the end through all disguises. The
Greeks told it as the tale of Perseus and
Andromeda ; they made their hero purely
Greek, a triumphant young son of immortal
Zeus, who rescues a beautiful princess, with
fair nude limbs like Parian marble, from the
devouring sea-monster. Mediæval Italy made
the sign of the cross, turned the son of
Danaë into a Christian martyr, and clad the
beautiful nude maiden in clinging silk robes,
as it would fain have clad Melian Aphrodite
herself when it converted her image into a
crowned Madonna. The Renaissance came,
and Cellini unclothed her again, in his revived
paganism, to set her polished bronze limbs,
where every eye might see and stare, in the
Piazza at Florence. Our modern novelists
dress her up afresh in the princess robe of
the day (sage green or crushed strawberry),
and turn her loose on that slimy old dragon
the world, till Prince Charming comes by,
as a baronet in a tennis suit, to lay at her
feet ten thousand a year and the title of My
Lady. But 'tis the old tale still, and who
lists to tell it may trick it out once more in
his own heart's fashion. For though there
be nothing new under the sun, the old wonder

is there, as marvellous as ever, if you choose
to marvel at it. Each spring brings it back,
a perpetual miracle.

So I set forth into the world, a Princess
Cleodolind of the nineteenth century, ready
to face the dragons that, as I well know,
abound in it, and full of faith in the St. George
who will come to rescue me. I mean to sail
away on my Odyssey, unabashed, touching
at such shores as may chance to beckon, yet
hopeful of reaching at last the realms of
Alcinous.

From all which you may guess that I am
a Girton girl.

CHAPTER II.

THE STRUGGLE FOR LIFE.

You may guess it, I say; for it is no part of my plan to tell you. Being a woman, I throw out this hint to pique your curiosity.

Let us return to the point that I was twenty-two, and had no employment. Commissioner Lin and I were alone and friendless.

Four months earlier I had suffered a great loss. How great a loss I am not careful to assure you. It is far from my desire to make capital out of my inmost heart. I cannot spin phrases about my dead father. But by this time the first fierce numbness of my sorrow had worn away; I was no longer a stone; I was beginning to smile, and to feel the sunshine. A certain quicksilver light-heartedness in the veins of my race helps to conceal a background of feeling. Besides, I had my livelihood to earn. That is a great resource. The need for bread served to edge out my grief. My first four months had been assured me beforehand in the Settlement; for we paid in advance, half-yearly, our Warden being a prudent soul who disliked bad debts, and preferred the safe side. But when the four months of my deepest mourning were over, it was absolutely necessary for me to find employment.

How it all came about I need not inform you : the bank that broke, the electric light that failed : I was told the details in terms so crabbed that if I tried to repeat them I could but show my ignorance.

It was not hard for me to be poor; for in the Settlement we lived as the other East-Enders live, and I had learned from my match-girls how to be hungry and merry. But my poverty hitherto had been that of the amateur; I had now to learn professional indigence. When I shook hands with Sister Phyllis and Sister Agatha at the door of the guild, leaving Commissioner Lin in their charge for the moment, and went forth into the world to earn my living, I had six and elevenpence as available assets. I was a capitalist in my way. That formed my capital.

"Under these circumstances," I said to myself, "the first thing for a prudent girl to

do is to look out for lunch ; the second thing
is to look out for a situation."

I do not pretend to prevision ; on the contrary, I was born to take no heed for the
morrow. I belong to the tribe of the grass-
hopper, not that of the ant. But I had been
so deeply impressed by Sister Phyllis's ex-
hortations during my last four months in the
guild that I had taken pains to learn shorthand and type-writing. I did not then know
that every girl in London can write shorthand, and that type-writing as an accom-
plishment is as diffused as the piano ; else
I might have turned my hand to some
honest trade instead, such as millinery or
cake-making. However, a type-writer I was,
and a type-writer I must remain. So I set
forth on my Odyssey by walking down the
phantom-haunted channel of the Strand, and
cast anchor for my first halt in an aërated
bread shop.

Luxury, we are told, demoralises this age,
and (while I remain a type-writer) I am absolute to set my face against it. But a cup
of coffee and a slice of seed-cake (not too
luxuriously sweetened) lay well within the
compass of my capital. I am a poor arith-
metician, but I arrive by finger-lore at the net

result that fourpence from six and elevenpence
leaves six and seven. I took up an evening
paper, which some recklessly extravagant cus-
tomer had bequeathed to his successors, and
my eye scanned the advertisements. Hands
that waved a signal seemed to catch my glance.
"A sail on the horizon!" I cried to myself.
And this is what I read—

"Shorthand and Type-writer wanted
(female). Legal work.—Apply Flor and
Fingelman, 27B, Southampton Row."

I felt myself already on the road to fortune.
A glance at the date: it was to-day's paper!
In matters of business, promptitude is everything. I would be the first to apply. I tossed
off my hot coffee with unbecoming haste, and,
deeply impressed with the fact that in this
age the struggle for existence has become one
of the rights of woman, I hurried with all
speed to Flor and Fingelman's.

I was a Shorthand and Type-writer
(female); and I was fully prepared to be as
legal as they desired of me.

I do not say that "female" is a poetical
description. I have never heard it applied
to Heloise or to Ophelia—not even by the
grave-digger; though Touchstone, to be sure,
uses it once of Audrey. But the nineteenth

century has a chivalry all its own, which I scruple to depreciate. If it speaks of us as females, it has given us the bicycle, and it almost admits that we are as fit for the franchise as the forty-shilling lodger. It puts us a little lower than the navvies. I call that magnanimity.

I had made haste to run up Charing Cross Road, and when I reached Southampton Row, impressed by the importance of the Struggle for Existence, I believe I was absolute winner in the race against time for the position of Shorthand and Type-writer (female).

Up two pair of stairs, where a notice led, I entered the Outer Office. Its keynote was fustiness. Three clerks (male), in seedy black coats, the eldest with hair the colour of a fox's, went on chaffing one another for two minutes after I closed the door, with ostentatious unconsciousness of my insignificant presence.

No doubt they inferred that I was a candidate for the post of Shorthand and Type-writer (female), and they treated me as such persons may look to be treated. Their talk turned upon that noble animal, the horse.

They spoke also of the turf; by which I understood them to allude, not so much to

the greensward of the downs, as to the imperceptible moral turf of Fleet Street. The
two younger were indeterminate young men,
with straight black hair, and features modelled
on an oyster's. As they appeared to be
loftily unaware of my intrusion, I signified my
presence by coughing slightly. It was the
apologetic cough that stands for " I beg your
pardon, but will you kindly attend to me ? "
They did not permit even the cough, however, to hurry them unduly. The youngest
of the three, a pulpy youth, adjusted his
cuffs, and completed some deep remarks upon
two-year-old form before he turned to stare
at me. I suppose he was kind enough to be
satisfied with my personal appearance, for
after a while he wheeled round on his high
stool, and broke out with the chivalry of his
age and class, "Well, what's your business?"

My voice trembled a little, but I mustered
up courage and spoke. " I have called about
your advertisement for a Shorthand and
Type-writer (female)."

He eyed me up and down. I am slender,
and, I will venture to say, if not pretty, at
least interesting-looking.

" How many words a minute ? " he asked
after a long pause.

I stretched truth as far as its elasticity
would permit. "One ninety-seven," I answered with an affectation of the precisest
accuracy. To say "Two hundred" were commonplace.

The pulpy youth ran his eyes over me as
if I were a horse for sale. I was conscious
of my little black dress and hat; conscious
also of a fiery patch in the centre of my
cheek; but if you struggle for life you must expect these episodes. "That's good enough,"
he said slowly, with a side-glance at his
fellow-clerks. I had a painful suspicion that
the words were intended rather for them
than for me, and that they bore reference
more to my face and figure than to my real
or imagined pace per minute.

The eldest clerk, with the foxy head,
wheeled round, and took his turn to stare.
He had hairy hands and large goggle-eyes.

"Got your own machine?" he asked.

"Yes."

"What sort?"

"A Barlock."

"That'll do," he said, eyeing the rest. And
again I detected an undercurrent of double
meaning. He seemed to be expressing modi-
fied satisfaction at my outer personality.

They questioned me for some minutes with equal grace and charm. Then the eldest rose slowly. "I'll tell the governor," he murmured, and disappeared through a dingy door marked in large letters "Mr. Fingelman."

In a short time he came back and beckoned me mysteriously. I followed him, trembling. He waved his hairy hand towards me as if to show me off to the man at the table. I felt disagreeably like Esther in the presence of Ahasuerus—a fat and oily Ahasuerus of fifty. "This is the young person," he said, by way of introduction.

Ahasuerus — otherwise Mr. Fingelman — inspected me in turn. I quailed before his glance; he was a commissioner for oaths, and wore large round spectacles. "Had experience?" he asked at last. In person he was rotund and obviously wealthy, though 'twas a third-rate solicitor's.

"A little," I replied. I had made up my mind to say "Lots" beforehand; but when it came to the pinch, the ingrained bad habit of speaking the truth reasserted itself partially.

Ahasuerus stared. "What name?" he asked, after a long stony gaze.

c

I stammered out " Juliet Appleton."

" Age ? "

" Twenty-two."

He perused me up and down with his small pig's-eyes, as if he were buying a horse, scrutinising my face, my figure, my hands, my feet. I felt like a Circassian in an Arab slave-market. I thought he would next proceed to examine my teeth. But he did not. Having satisfied himself as to externals, he went on to put me through my paces.

" S. down there," he said, pointing to a seat. "Have you pen and note-book ? " I produced my stylograph.

He grunted approbation, and dictated for a few minutes a short business-letter. Then he waved me to the type-writer. " Transcribe," he said curtly. I sat down and transcribed.

The chief clerk meanwhile stood by, with his hairy hands crossed in a curved attitude of ostentatious servility, which contrasted strangely with his Outer Office manner. When I had finished, he peered at my work, nodded, and handed it over to Ahasuerus. Ahasuerus ran his eye up and down, grunting again. " She'll do ? " he said interrogatively.

The chief clerk signed *yes*.

"She's the first we've seen," Ahasuerus interposed, with caution in his tone.

"Saves trouble," said the chief clerk. I was aware with a rush of hot blood that the chief clerk approved of me, and that to his lordly approbation (as of the Sultan's Vizier) I owed my appointment.

The Oriental monarch waved his pen towards the door. "Very well," he answered. "Settle terms with her outside. You know what I give. Bother me no more with it." And wheeling round his swivel-chair, he buried himself in his writing.

The terms the Vizier proposed were not wholly superior to the dreams of avarice; but they were a modest starvation; and after my East-End experiences, I looked for no more. I accepted them without demur, and went forth into Southampton Row an engaged type-writer.

I have a mercurial temperament. My spirits rise and fall as if they were consols. This success exalted me. I walked down Charing Cross Road (by no means, as a rule, an exhilarating thoroughfare) in the seventh heaven. I had justified myself before the impartial tribunal of political economy. I could earn my own bread—butter doubtful. In the Struggle for Life I had obtained a footing. This magnificent post of Shorthand and Type-writer (female) had been thrown open by adver-tisement to public competition. In that compe-tition I had won the day. My energy, my promptitude, the rapid resolution with which I had gulped down my coffee, burnt my tongue, and rushed off to Southampton Row, had se-cured for me the prize of a modest starvation. I had proved myself fittest by the mere fact of survival. Matthew Arnold had taught me, indeed, with much sweet reasonableness, that there was not any proper reason for my exist-ing; but I like to exist. The sole remaining question was, Could I adapt myself to my en-vironment? If so, I had fulfilled the whole gospel of Darwinism.

CHAPTER III.

ENVIRONMENT WINS.

IT was a wrench to tear myself away from my old men and women in the Isle of Dogs, for I truly loved them. The operation left a scar that was slow to heal. I felt I did them good : my visits cheered them, unlike the curate's ; my whimsical talk broke the monotony of old age and the East-End. But doing good is a luxury, and I was now face to face with the strict necessity of earning my livelihood. Yet hope lies still at the bottom of Pandora's box. Though I had but six and sevenpence in the world, and starvation wages, I started blithely to my work at Flor and Fingelman's.

I had found a room meanwhile to which my purse consented. The normal difficulties of lodging-hunting had been aggravated in my case by the need for finding a house where I should not be separated from Commissioner Lin ; which made a back-yard a necessity : but I succeeded in surmounting them. Commissioner Lin, I may say, to allay your fears, is my mongrel Chinese bull-pup. Like Ulysses, I have a dog ; he is ugly, but *a beauty*, and, oh, such a dear ! I may starve, but the Commissioner shares my last crust.

Geographically, my post was in the Outer Office. Early each morning I went in to the inner recess of Shushan the palace to receive Ahasuerus's instructions, and to take down from his royal lips my shorthand notes, which I afterwards expanded on the type-writer in the anteroom. Ahasuerus was graciously pleased to like me. I found favour, also, in the eyes of the Grand Vizier ; he was good enough to say my work was intelligent. I had doubts in my own mind as to the Vizier's competence to form an opinion on this head ; but was he not a man—a vote-wielding citizen, empowered to take his share (vicariously) in the counsels of the nation ? and was not I but a Shorthand and Type-writer (female) ? I bowed to the wisdom of the superior sex, and answered with a modest blush that I rejoiced to have earned his approval.

The morning and afternoon were taken up in expanding letters and copying drafts of documents. Their style was execrable. The principal verb adroitly concealed itself: the

principal adjective was usually "aforesaid."
Now, regarded as an epithet, I find "aforesaid" colourless. Its monotony bored me. I
suggested to Ahasuerus that his prose might
be enriched by a greater variety of graphic
adjectives such as "amethystine," "prismatic,"
"opalescent," "empyrean," or even "colos-
sal;" but he stared at me coldly, and replied
in a curt voice that legal phraseology was
necessarily limited. The Grand Vizier, also,
cavalierly rejected my mild suggestions for an
enlarged vocabulary. He contended that I
should model my composition on *Chitty on
Contract*. He was right, of course; but I
found the iteration of "provided always" in
that well of legal English intensely irksome.

The anteroom where I clicked was shared
by the Grand Vizier and the two other clerks.
They talked incessantly; I was forced to continue my transcription without interruption,
in spite of their voices. I will admit that
their discourse, as such, by no means distracted me, in virtue either of its intrinsic
attractiveness or of the nature of its subjects.
It circled chiefly round the noble quadruped,
with divergences on Rugby and Association
football. I did not gather that the Vizier and
his satellites knew much at first hand about

the breed of race-horses, nor could they have distinguished with ease between a fet-lock and a cannon-bone. They loved sport from afar : they were platonically horsey. But they were diligent students of a daily journal in the interest of manly pastimes : and they extracted from its pages many charming speculations as to the numerical chance of first and second favourites. They also spoke freely of the ladies of the music-hall. As their tongues rippled on, with peculiar London variants on the vowels of our native language, my type-writer continued to go click, click, click, till I was grateful for its sound as a counter-irritant to their inanity.

That click, click, click became to me like music—if only because it drowned the details of the Lewes Spring Meeting. I saw in it all a trail of Ibsenesque atavism. The horse was the sacred beast of the English in the days of Woden, and, in spite of St. Augustine and John Wesley, his worship still survives, its festivals attracting thousands of pilgrims each year to the centres of the cult at Epsom and Newmarket. Devotees may be known by their badge, a pink paper, which blushes itself, and is a cause of blushing in others.

Another peculiarity of the Outer Office was

its richness in dust—the dust specific to a solicitor's premises. I think, in this age of sanitation, I have kept my head tolerably unprejudiced on the subject of germs ; I do not speak evil of bacteria with the reckless extravagance of the world at large ; I am prepared to live and let live; nor do I deny to the bacilli of typhoid fever the common right to the struggle for existence. But the bacilli at Flor and Fingelman's, I must admit, were obtrusively aggressive. They carried the war into Africa. They flew about me visibly whenever I lifted a book ; they settled in myriads on my poor black dress ; they invaded my hair, and required to be daily dislodged by violent hostilities. The three clerks seemed to me to disregard them altogether ; and when I ventured timidly to suggest a duster, they were almost as horrified as when I proposed to vary the bald language of a writ by the introduction of a few graceful chromatic adjectives. Fustiness and mustiness are part of the profession, it seems ; you must no more attempt to sweep the Augean stables than to carry out that other Herculean task —the simplifying and codification of the law of England.

For three mornings and three afternoons I

endured Flor and Fingelman's. It was a
question of self *versus* environment. I am a
unit of the proletariat, and dear Sister Agatha
had impressed upon me often, with her sad,
sweet smile, the fundamental truth that beg-
gars must not be choosers. So I continued
to click, click, click, like a machine that I was,
and to listen as little as possible to the calcu-
lated odds upon King Arthur for the Ascot
Cup, till I was tired of the subject. On the
fourth day, however, the rebel in my blood
awoke. Not for nothing had my fathers
fought at Lexington. I felt I must strike one
blow for freedom. The aforesaid office failed
to respond to the needs of the party of the
first part. I went out to lunch, half resolved
in the whirligig I call my mind never to go
back again.

It was not the Grand Vizier, with his hairy
hands, his goggle eyes, and his false diamonds;
though a certain insolent condescension in the
creature's manner made me shrink from his
presence. It was not the junior clerks; though
the tone of voice with which they addressed
me as "Miss" reminded me of the accent
in which I had often heard men of their type
bespeak a defenceless barmaid; while their
demeanour varied from the haughty to the

condescending. It was Ahasuerus himself
whose Oriental leer drove me from the office.
I felt sure Ahasuerus considered his manner
killing—a three-tailed bashaw, with a natural
gift of captivating Circassians. His smile was
the smile that knows itself irresistible. He
had not as yet ventured anything rude to me ;
but I scented prospective rudeness in the way
he watched me come in and out—the way he
beamed on me benignly, with his small pig's-
eyes, as who should say, " See how bland and
how pleasant I am ; you must rejoice, mere
female, to have secured the favour of so genial
a gentleman, who revels in semi-detached
affluence at Balham." I fled from his oily face,
assured that the law was not my proper
sphere. I would diverge into paths of more
commonplace business.

All this time I had been living upon Capital. If you judge such conduct imprudent,
remember that I could hardly have lived upon
its interest. My six and sevenpence was
almost spent. I owed my landlady (at the
single room I had taken) for bread and rent.
I had nothing left for my own food or for Mr.
Commissioner. The outlook was serious.
Dimly aware of failure in the Struggle for
Life—inability to succeed in Adaptation to the

Environment—I retired for lunch to a little shop close by, whose merits the Grand Vizier had from the first impressed upon me.

At the table by my side sat two middle-aged men. They were talking earnestly. I detected at once in the mellow tone of the better-looking of the two that he was a Cambridge man and a political economist. The Moral Sciences Tripos has its special aroma. After the rippling tittle-tattle of the noble quadruped I was glad to listen even to the voice of economics. I strained my ears. It was pleasant to hear educated men speak again. And their talk was full of interest.

"You have been to see them?" the first voice said.

"Yes," the Cambridge man answered. "It is an interesting experiment, though fore-doomed to failure. They say they want to try anarchy in practice. They have bought ten acres of wild land very cheap; they are getting it into tillage; and they mean to manage it upon Kropotkine's system of intensive culture."

Intensive culture! I saw at once what that meant. What a capital plan! Till the land to the utmost, so as to make the largest possible amount of food or roses come out of it. And anarchists, too! Why, I was born an anarchist. Never could I endure being ordered about by anyone. After Flor and Fingelman's—click, click, click, all day—what a vista of Eden! I sat a postulant at the gate of that Paradise. Just to go out into the fields and till them anarchically!

"And have they no organisation?"

"None at all. He told me it was a band of brothers. I asked him by what rule they worked. He said each man or woman laboured when he or she chose! If he didn't feel inclined he left off for that day and sat in the sun, basking. They cultivate in common; each member of the community receives food and clothes; and at the end of the week, if any surplus remain, they divide it between them by way of pocket-money."

"Then it acts, so far."

"Yes, apparently. But 'tis new. They look healthy enough, though pallid, and they are certainly enthusiastic. I asked Rothenburg how he liked it; he said it was delightful—ten thousand times better than being a tailor in Paris."

I could no longer restrain myself. A caprice seized me. I leaned across the table. "Pardon me," I said, "but may I venture to ask, as an anarchist in the grain, where shall I find this Utopia, this Eldorado of anarchy ? "

The Cambridge man smiled.

" Near Horsham," he answered. " But— excuse curiosity — are you *really* an anarchist ? "

" I will join them ! " I cried, clasping my hands. " I have every qualification. I am alone in the world, and penniless—splendid material for anarchy. Such idyllic anarchy, too ! Do they receive mere women ? "

" I think," the Cambridge man replied, "they would be charmed to take you. But remember, they are uncultivated—the raw material of a state, rough working men and women. Go down and see them by all means. But when you have inspected their home I venture to hazard a guess that you will decide it is not meant for ladies."

" I am young," I answered ; " I have tolerable strength and abundant energy. Misfortunes are nothing if one takes them in the spirit of camping out. Hardships cease to be hardships when you talk of them as roughing it. After all, it is only what we voluntarily do at a picnic up the river. At least, I will go down and interview your anarchists."

He scribbled their precise address on the back of an envelope, with a smile for my enthusiasm. I went home to my solitary room at once, and sat down to my private and particular Barlock—the same on which I am inditing these present memoirs—to write out my resignation to Flor and Fingelman.

"GENTLEMEN,

"WHEREAS I, the undersigned, have worked for three days and upwards, be the same more or less, to my great discomfort, in your dingy, stingy, musty, and fusty office ; and WHEREAS I have found the post of Shorthand and Type-writer (female) which you have deigned to bestow upon me, in the aforesaid office, highly disagreeable to my mind and brain, owing as well to the impurity of the air as to the dulness and monotony of the terms employed in it ; and WHEREAS I am now desirous of seeking other and more congenial employment elsewhere than in the aforesaid dinginess, stinginess, mustiness, and fustiness, as herein designated, NOW THEREFORE, This Indenture Witnesseth and know all men by these presents, that I have made up my mind not to return to your messuage or tenement this afternoon, nor on any subsequent date, but to relinquish entirely the aforesaid post of Shorthand and Type-writer (female) with all and sundry the emoluments or salaries thereto pertaining, and to say good-bye to you, the aforesaid Flor and Fingelman, and to your Grand Vizier and other faithful satellites. In witness whereof I have hereto set my hand and seal, this twenty-first day of May, in the year of our Lord, &c., &c.

"JULIET APPLETON."

I put it into an envelope and dropped it into the post; then I turned again on my way, a Free Woman.

Free, but penniless.

Hurrah for anarchy! flowery, bowery anarchy, in a careless-ordered garden, run wild with eglantine! Could a Peri hope to storm that Eden?

CHAPTER IV.

THE CHOICE OF A PATRON.

I PROWLED along the Strand, in quest of an inspiration. You will readily conceive that the situation was serious. I had disbursed my last coin for lunch that morning. True, I had still my bicycle ; and by its aid I might set off to join my unknown brothers, the anarchists, near Horsham. But my heart smote me, for I had not wherewith to pay my landlady. Had I worked out my week with Ahasuerus, no doubt I might have settled her bill, and gone on my way honestly. But I could not leave her in the lurch ; nor, indeed, could I set out without the contents of my modest portmanteau. My effects must go with me. Thus the position teemed with difficulties. I had an aunt in London, of course ; I suppose not even the most destitute are ever wholly deprived of the solace of a maiden aunt in London. Conscience suggested that in such a crisis I ought to consult her. But fortunately I belong to a generation which has analysed conscience away. "Go to the aunt," said Duty. "Stop away," said Inclination. And Inclination, as usual, won in a canter—I might almost say, Inclination walked over. If you doubt that these metaphors are becoming on a woman's lips, you must recollect that my style had been suffering for three days from the enforced proximity of the Grand Vizier, his satraps, and the noble quadruped.

I *could* not go to the aunt. She was the average woman of the small fixed income; prosaic, stagnant, serenely literal; a placid pool that reflects its surroundings. It was her fixed belief that everything I did was in equal parts foolish and wicked. No doubt she was right; but her arguments vexed me. " It is quite impossible for a young lady to do so," she said about many actions which I knew from experience to be not only possible but actual. So I avoided the aunt, and set my face toward the shop-windows for light and guidance. I found it, of course. Faith is always rewarded, or I like to think so. At a corner shop, devoted to the sale of more or less genuine *bric-à-brac*, I saw in the window a charming little Fra Angelico, almost a replica of a miniature I remembered to have noted at the Vatican. Whether it was authentic or not I do not presume to decide ; who am I that I should give myself the airs of a Morelli ? But its *naïveté*, its grace, its frank purity of colour, were obvious at once, even to the eye of a woman. The picture represented what is called in art the Charity of St. Nicholas. Through an open door you see into the home of a poor nobleman. 'Tis a dainty interior, of the age when drab had not wholly ousted the primary hues. In the background his three starving daughters lie snugly in bed—a trio of innocent maidens, with pretty blonde heads of infantile guilelessness, laid on white pillows, between dimity curtains. In the foreground the nobleman their father is seated, the picture of despair, in a long vermilion robe and a brown study ; without, by a grated window, the dear young saint himself, in Florentine hose, with a sleeveless jerkin, stands timidly on tip-toe, in the very act of dropping three purses of gold as dowries for the maidens through the open casement. The story is told with the pellucid simplicity of early Tuscan art ; no airs and graces, but just the bare outline of facts which it behoves you to know ; — these girls are

D 2

poor ; their father is at his wits' end ; and
yonder amiable young gentleman, in crimson
and puce, has come to their rescue, like a
gallant Christian, with purses of gold very fat
and opulent.

I stood long and looked at it. It was so
archly engaging. The clear-cut outlines, the
translucent hues, the sweet old-world direct-
ness, the story-telling faculty, each charmed
and beguiled me. "After all," I said to myself, "St. Nicholas, not St. George, is the
saint for me. My dragon is poverty. St.
George for princesses ; St. Nicholas for the
poor and portionless maiden ! " I gazed at
him long, with affectionate eyes ; then I went
on my way towards the National Gallery,
strengthened and comforted.

Have you found out the true use of the
National Gallery, I wonder ? On three days
in the week the British nation throws those
stately rooms open, free, to any woman who
chooses to enter them. I use them as my
drawing-room. You get a comfortable chair
to sit upon for nothing ; you get pictures to
look at ; and in winter the gallery is heated
by flues, over which you car stand and warm
your feet gratis. I went in on this critical
afternoon of my history, not only for rest, but

in search of St. Nicholas—St. Nicholas of
Myra—St. Nicholas of Bari—St. Nicholas,
the giver of dowries to damsels. My dear
father had been a lover of Italian art, and had
taught me betimes the legends of the saints,
without which Fra Angelico and Benozzo
Gozzoli talk a strange tongue to you. I was
certain now that St. Nicholas, not St. George,
was my predestined patron. He was so good
to the poor, and especially to maidens. In
many pictures on those walls I beheld him
as of old, in his bishop's robes, benign and
benevolent, a model of suavity, holding the
three golden balls which typify the three fat
purses of gold he threw in at the window to
the starving daughters of the nobleman of
Myra. He was the saint of the oppressed,
the enslaved, the suffering. If knighthood
had its St. George, serfdom had its St.
Nicholas. I saw him again, with his three
spheres of gold, traced by the hand of
Raphael in the Blenheim Madonna ; a courteous old gentleman here, bland and mild,
and very sweet of feature. I saw him in
many other less famous pictures, a friend in
need, ever gentle and helpful, the patron of
children, of the distressed, of the storm-tossed.
I saw him in many guises, painted for the

most part in what, in default of exact knowledge, I will call a chasuble, but always as the
deliverer.   My heart went forth to him.
" Holy Nicholas," I murmured, " you were
my father's friend ; be my friend as well !
Stand by me, and protect me ! "

I issued once more into the phantom-
crowded Strand.   Below, the streaming street
was full of those hurrying, scurrying men
with black bags, bound as ever for the Unknown.   But above—I lifted my eyes, and
there, clear against the sky, I beheld—the
three golden balls of St. Nicholas.

CHAPTER V.

I DREW a deep breath. He was the poor man's saint; his symbol has descended to the poor man's banker.

Yet my confidence after all was not all misplaced. St. Nicholas, at a pinch, would provide my dowry.

It flashed across me at a stroke what those golden balls meant. Never before had I divined their meaning—their intimate connection with my newly-chosen patron. I caught at it now clearly. Nicholas, I knew, was the saint of the people—the saint of the labourer who toils for daily bread, of the fisherman who struggles with the stormy sea, of the orphan, of the slave, of the child, the captive, the prisoner, the unfortunate. No wonder, then, that his golden balls have survived as the badge of that generous profession which freely lends to all the poor who leave a pledge behind.

I accepted the omen. Tempest-tossed as I was, my precious type-writer might save me for the day from the present distresses. I hurried back to my attic in a street off Soho, packed it up in its case, and carried it with difficulty in my own small arms to the shrine of St. Nicholas.

My errand, I grant, was new, and repugnant. But necessity, like our magistrates, knows no law. I will not pretend that I passed those dubious portals without a flush of shame. Still, I passed them bravely.

"How much?" asked the acolyte.

I was inexperienced in the ritual of the sordid temple. "Three pounds?" I queried tentatively.

He cut me short with a gesture of contempt. "We could do thirty shillings."

"I *paid* twenty pounds for it," I murmured.

He shrugged his shoulders. "An error of judgment, I should say. Thirty shillings. Do you take it?"

I was anxious to escape from the squalid place. Bundles of shabby clothes in square pigeon-holes daunted me. "I accept," I said, gasping. He counted out the money, and handed me a ticket.

I fled, like one followed by a roaring wild

beast. No quicker flies the Arimaspian whom the gryphon pursues. Nor did I pause or halt till I reached my own bower. Safe back in that stronghold, I bolted and locked the door, and washed the pollution off me in an orgy of cold water.

Then the dignity of womanhood reasserted itself. I sat back in the one arm-chair, and reflected. A freak is dear to my soul. I would pay my weekly bill before starting, carry my knapsack with me, and engage the room for another week in advance, in case the anarchists should chance to prove too anarchic for my taste. And after that, who dare call me imprudent ? 'Tis the habit of twenty-two to burn its boats. When it takes measures for preserving them, you should give it credit for singular forethought.

I had still my faithful bicycle. I rose betimes next morning, and endued myself in my cycling costume, which, like all else about me (I trust), is rational. The Commissioner and I stole silently down the stairs. Before London was well awake we had left Westminster Bridge behind us in the haze, and were off on the open road, on our way towards Horsham, two palmers bent for the Holy Land of Anarchy.

How light and free I felt! When man first set woman on two wheels with a pair of pedals, did he know, I wonder, that he had rent the veil of the harem in twain ? I doubt it ; but so it was. A woman on a bicycle has all the world before her where to choose ; she can go where she will, no man hindering. I felt it that brisk May morning as I span down the road, with a Tam o' Shanter on my head, and my loose hair travelling after me like a Skye terrier.

"This," thought I to myself, "is truly my Odyssey. To play at being a latter-day Ulysses in London, among those crowded streets, is like a child's game—too much make-believe. But mounted here on the ship of the high-road, scudding gaily down hill, or luffing against head-winds on a steep upward slope, I feel myself the heroine of a modern sea epic. As I coast by narrow straits of hedge-bordered lane, round some lumbering cart, I steer with care betwixt headland and whirlpool. Siren inns hang out signs to becken me into port ; piratical carts, bucca-neering drays, skidding fast down long slopes, strive to crush me as they pass like living Symplegades. In perils oft, I yet feel the fresh wind in my teeth, and see the foam

of May break over hawthorn promontories.
Troy lies behind ; in front of me beckons
the peaceful Ithaca of my anarchist settlement."

The road, indeed, was a pleasant one.
Lying at first among suburban quarters, pink
with blossom at that perfect moment of the
year, and heavy with lilac, it grew greener
by degrees as it stretched out to the rising
plain of Surrey and then swelled up slowly
into the great breaker of the chalk downs.
That huge wave of land rises in a long curve
on the side towards London, but curls over
abruptly by Box Hill and Dorking, like a
billow that has hardened in the act of breaking. My way led me through a deep gorge
that cuts the slope of this ridge at right
angles, beside a wandering stream, as though
one stroke of some great magician's wand
had cleft a way for it through the barrier.
The ravine is bordered to the left by a cliff-
like edge, overgrown with juniper bushes.
They call it the Vale of Mickleham. Spring
had put on her best frock for my visit. I
rode at a good pace. Commissioner Lin toiled
behind, with his tongue out. Then we broke
into the open, where a steeple showed the
way, and through a billowy common, crest

after trough alternately, dotted thick with holly-trees, across the Weald of Sussex. A still, pearly-pale sky hung over the misty level. Despondent donkeys munched furze-tops and mused pessimism. Trains dashed under bridges with long streamers of steam, as I rode over them unabashed—huge monsters of burnished brass, snorting death from their throats, such as would have terrified the timid Achæan sailors. But I took no heed of them—I, the braver daughter of an iron age, trained to disregard dragons of that mechanical sort, and to fear only those against whom St. Nicholas is potent—I had seen one but yesterday on Margaritone's panel. The horses that passed over by my side reared and quivered at the ungainly monster ; but my undaunted steel palfrey, himself a scion of the iron age, showed no sign of weakness. Or if he trembled at all, 'twas something wrong in the gearing.

A mile or two from Horsham I diverged, as directed, down a cross-road to the left. 'Twas a level lane in champaign country, bordered by a low hedge of close-clipped maple. The fields were of leaden clay— so much I saw where they were ploughed —muddy, and all but impassable in wet

weather, to meet which state of morass every
cottage was approached by a small paved
causeway of flags, giving a singularly distinc-
tive note to the district.   Many such I passed,
each built of pale red brick, each tiled with
mossy tiles, and each approached through a
square of front garden by its town-like pavement.   The lanes were a maze, running aim-
lessly hither and thither.   One after another,
as I tried it, led me back by circumvolutions
to a rustic Clapham Junction, the centre of
Nowhere.   Judge if I was nonplussed.

At one of the cottages I reined up at last,
and, leaning from my saddle, called out to a
boy who was weeding the front patch : " Can
you tell me where I shall find the anarchist
settlement ? "

The boy looked up, taken aback.   It was
clear that the rationality of my dress astonished him.   And, indeed, 'tis so rare to be
rational in this world that I was not surprised
at his surprise.   He stared at me with a
frank provincial stare ; I am not sure that
he did not design heaving half a brick at
me, in recognition of my originality.   But he
contented himself with a few contumelious
epithets, which did not hurt me.   I flung him
a penny ; this softened his heart.   He an-

swered, after a pause, " I guess you mean them furriners."

The American blood in me was flattered by that " I guess." Thus my ancestors must have spoken here in Sussex long ago, before they went over in the *Mayflower*, to fight in due time at Lexington. It is a point of honour with all Massachusetts folk to have gone over in the *Mayflower*. She was a sloop of 180 tons, and must have carried thousands of steerage passengers. I am not sure about the tonnage, but there can be no doubt as to the passengers.

" They are probably foreigners," I replied, coming back to this century. " At any rate, they are new-comers. And I was told they had settled down somewhere near Pinfold."

He waved his hand vaguely towards the quarter of the sunrise, and gave me directions of complicated topography. But he added, after a moment for internal reflection, " They bain't the sort o' folk for the likes o' you to visit."

" Thank you," I answered, "I am an anarchist myself." And I spurred on my mount, round the corner where he directed me.

The day, which was brisk when I started,

had become by this time hot and windless, and the sun beat mercilessly. After various intricate twists and turns, ill-deciphered from uncertain instructions, I found myself at last by the side of a pond which formed the one fixed point in my guide's geography. He had called it "a horse-pond." It was a pretty little pool : tall glossy weeds grew lush by its edge ; a grey-leaved willow drooped into it ; Naiads lurked among the broad green disks of the water-lilies at its farther end. I was glad it was so taking. I accepted it as an omen of success in my wild-goose chase. From the first I was not without misgivings of my own wisdom in thus seeking to frater- nise with unknown anarchist brethren. But I knew how often fortune brings in some boats that are not steered ; and I took the beauty of this "horse-pond" as a foretaste of what I should find in the anarchist settle- ment.

An old woman, with sleeves tucked up and the parboiled arms of a laundress, stood near the door of a new brick cottage hard by. "Can you tell me," I called out, "where I can find Rothenburg ? "

I omitted the Mr., as my Cambridge friend had warned me that that harmless prefix acted on your anarchist like the picador's dart on the bulls of Andalusia.

"Rottenborough?" the old woman answered, transforming his name, as is the wont of her class, into something significant in her own language. "He's down yonder by the new glass-house." And she pointed with her hand towards a deep clay field just behind her cottage.

I dismounted, and led my bicycle gently through the mud. There was no eglantine. At the far end of the field, under shelter of a hedge which backed it to the north, I saw a slender, pale-faced young man in a blue Continental blouse, digging a trench with a pick, to whose use he was evidently but little accustomed.

"Are you Rothenburg?" I asked, in French.

He looked up and smiled. My costume took his fancy. "I am," he answered in the same language, but with a marked Alsatian accent. "What do you want with me, comrade?"

"I am an anarchist," I said, simply, rushing straight to the point. "I wish to join your community."

He laid down his pick, and came up out of

the trench. I could see him better now—
a pallid, anæmic young man, with a high
narrow forehead, watery restless eyes, thin
yellow hair, and twitching hands that played
nervously all the time with a shadowy moustache. I judged him at sight the very type of
an eager-hearted ineffectual enthusiast—a man
born to failure as the sparks fly upward.

He looked me over, all surprised. "We
are a party of working men," he objected, at
last; "artisans, sempstresses, labourers. We
do not desire or court the aid of the *bourgeois*."

Now, I can endure most things, but not
to be called a *bourgeoise*. I coloured a little,
I suppose ; at any rate, I answered, "I am
an *ouvrière* myself. I have nothing to do
with the *bourgeoisie*. I have ridden down from
London to link my fate with yours. Are
you the head of this colony?"

He flushed somewhat in turn—or rather,
faint streaks of pink stole over that bloodless
face. "We have no head," he answered.
"We are thorough-going anarchists. Equality
is our aim. Since when do you belong to
our party?"

"Since I was born," I retorted, boldly.
"I am anarchic by nature. Wherever there

E

is a government, I am always against it.   Let
me join your band—and I promise dis-
obedience."

He eyed me suspiciously.   This confession
of faith seemed rather to disturb than to
reassure him.   He paused a moment.   "How
did you hear of us ?"

"Casually, in an eating-house in London,
from a Cambridge economist who had been
here to see you.   When he spoke of you,
I thought to myself, ' These are the people
I want.   I recognise my kind.   I must go
and join them.'"

"Ha!   He was a co-operator.   A voluntary
co-operator.   But he had not the whole truth.
If he sent you here, you may be wrong—you
are perhaps a Marxian ? "

I perceived that there was an orthodoxy
and a heterodoxy of anarchism ; in which case,
of course, I should be on the heterodox side.
"You will find me sound," I said, seeking to
temporise, " in my uncompromisingly anarchic
anarchism of anarchy."   I thought I could
hardly be more mutinous than that.   If 'twas
rebellion they wanted, I was honestly prepared to rebel against the rebels.

He drew out a cheap gun-metal watch.
" It is dinner-time," he said, temporising in

return. "The comrades will have assembled. Come up and discuss. We will see whether they are content to accept you as a companion."

I confess I was disappointed. This seemed painfully close to a legislative assembly—at the very least to a folk-moot or parish council. Did they mean to decide things by base show of hands? And if so, wherein did your anarchist differ from the ordinary coercive governmental authority?

In the Utopia I had framed for myself, every man (or woman) did that which was right in his own eyes—without prejudice to his equal freedom to do that which was wrong, if he chanced to be so minded. Here, I saw just a common joint-stock company— Anarchy, Limited.

CHAPTER VI.

THE INNER BROTHERHOOD.

WE assembled in the large room of the first cottage I had seen—a sort of bare, bald dining-hall, big enough to feed some twenty or thirty souls, and ugly enough to take away their appetite for ever. Its architect's name, I would conjecture, was Jeremiah.

"A new comrade," Rothenburg said, waving his hand towards me not ungracefully. "Let us dine first, and consider her afterward."

This was an awkward introduction. I sat down to eat and drink, painfully conscious that the eyes of anarchic Europe were upon me. My long unbroken ride had given me a keen edge for food ; still, apart from their scrutiny, I confess I eat with an undercurrent of disgust. The meat and bread were wholesome; but I suspected their cleanliness. The napery, too, was coarse and cried for the laundress. However, if one chooses to

herd with anarchists, one must not be too
particular on matters of diet. I eat a hearty
dinner, in spite of my doubts, and even drank
some sour red wine ; for they were not
English enough yet to relish our beer, of
which I was not sorry.

Replenished by dinner, they drew apart,
discussing me in low tones and in cosmopoli-
tan languages. I fancy I detected the ring
both of Czech and Yiddish—tongues of which
I do not profess an intimate knowledge, though
my East-End experiences had given me a
distant nodding acquaintance with either.
Most of them were Austrians (assorted) or
else subjects of the Tsar, living here for their
health, because they preferred England as a
place of residence to that part of the Russian
territory which is called Siberia. From time
to time they appealed to me on some point
of my history—where was I born, of what
nationality, why did I wish to join them ? I
answered as best I might, though the ordeal
was severe. It was bad enough to stand as
Esther before Ahasuerus, but I realised now
that I was set to perform the part of Vashti
before a whole court of critical anarchists.

At last Rothenburg, still fumbling with his
moustache, had the happy thought to ask me

my name. When I said "Juliet Appleton" I
saw that it moved them. The fact that I was
a Juliet gave food to their fancy. Each man
drew himself up and stroked his chin with the
very air of a Romeo. Even the women smiled
—for there were women among them, some
four or five, with pretty curly-haired children.
Then they began to instruct me in the doc-
trines of their sect. I was sworn to eternal
friendship with all and sundry. The intricate
Eleusinian mysteries of anarchy were explained
to me, as catechumen, in Alsatian French and
Bohemian German. I answered in such dia-
lects of either tongue as I had at command.
My profession of faith appeared to give satisfaction, especially when, prompted by Rothenburg, I renounced Karl Marx and all his ways,
and embraced with fervour the true faith of
Bakunin. Who or what Bakunin was I had
not an idea : but I made up in zeal what I
lacked in understanding.

It began to dawn on me that sectarianism
is of the nature of man, and that all things
tend to fall into my doxy and your doxy.

At last Rothenburg arrived at what he
evidently considered a crucial point in his
catechism. " You understand, of course, that
you must not form an idolatrous attachment

to any one of the comrades, to the exclusion of the others?"

I glanced around me at the dozen sorry specimens of the male of my species there ranged before me, and felt convinced at sight I could safely engage not to idolise excessively any one among them. And I said so.

This assurance appeared to give the community boundless satisfaction. They turned next to my bicycle, which was a nice little machine—the nicest in England, indeed, like everyone else's. One or two of them were kind enough to accept my full membership at once by trying to ride it. I am tolerably tall for a woman, while the comrades, as I learned to call them, were for the most part under-sized town-bred working men, of the skimpy order. Thus my machine just fitted them; they did not even require to shift the pedals. I showed them how to stick on, correcting the excessive line of grace in their initial curves : this obviously pleased them, and I think they formed a high idea of the new comrade herself and more especially of the property she brought into the Community. They had not an equal opinion of Mr. Commissioner.

So I settled down at once as a full-fledged anarchist.

Figure to yourself a group of naked cottages, with bald slate roofs untempered by the years—no moss, no house-leeks—dropped down at random in a sticky clay cabbage-field —and you see our colony.

My first business was to behold where I was to abide. The rotund old lady whom I had found at the door of the first messuage or tenement took me round to my cubicle; for they had a nomenclature of their own, suited to the ways of anarchists. 'Twas in a brand-new building of pale pink brick—a sort of anæmic brick, which bore the same relation to healthy red brickiness that Rothenburg's complexion bore to normal humanity. It was vastly modern, like the views of its builders; it also betrayed the same painful lack of æsthetic tendencies. It cried for creepers. In front of it stretched a patch of utilitarian potato-ground. I would have preferred holly-hocks. There was no hall or passage: the door opened abruptly into a small parlour; behind lay three bedrooms of the minutest dimensions. Mine was tiny. However, I have always inculcated kindness to animals, and am not conscious of the faintest desire to swing a cat; so it sufficed very well for me. The bath entailed difficulties, no other anar-

chist being a slave to the habit; but a wooden
water-tub and economy of space speedily over-
came them. I unpacked my knapsack, put my
room to rights, dusted the window-panes, and
sallied forth to see what work the Community
demanded of me.

The Community was ranged outside my
cottage door as one man. It seemed that,
unable to resist the combined attractions of
the bicycle and a new comrade, they had
decreed a half-holiday by universal suffrage,
and were waiting without to let me teach
them the use of the machine. But the Commissioner, who was an unregenerate monopolist as to private property, effectually prevented
its premature appropriation by a mute white
protest.

I trembled as I saw how many awkward
youths desired to ride my precious cycle.
But if you go in for Communism you must
expect it to cut both ways. I had eaten their
dinner, they must share my bicycle. For so
it is written in the lawless law of anarchy.

Most of these young men were good fel-
lows in their way—very simple-hearted anarchists. I do not credit it that they could have
blown up a Tsar, or even dropped a bomb into
a suburban letter-box. They confined them-

selves to cabbages and passionate denuncia-
tion of the oppressors. But the ringleader
in the attempt to borrow my bicycle from an
absent comrade was an exception to the rule.
He was a villainous-looking creature—the
Caliban of our island. His name was Léon.
I think he must have been built after designs
by Mr. Aubrey Beardsley. He had rufous hair,
a nose without a bridge, and thick protruding
lips. Those lips were a nightmare. I set
him down as a judicious cross between a
Swiss *crétin* and an albino negro. To make
matters worse, like many other repulsive
people, he had the habit when he spoke
to you of coming up very close and breathing
in your face, so that his protruding lips almost
seemed to touch you. I had an irresistible impulse to say to him, "Take, oh take those lips
away!" only, I knew if I did he would not
understand ; or if he understood he would
misunderstand me.

I felt from the outset that I might have
trouble with Léon.

That first night, for some time, I was kept
awake by a continuous concert, which sorely
puzzled me. It could not be nightingales—
the note was not varied enough ; nor was it
the Six Great Powers of Europe—the chorus

was far too concordant. It reminded me most of the serenade made by the small green southern tree-frogs; but here, in Sussex! I lay awake and racked my brain. Next day solved the mystery. The hollow beyond our plot of intensive culture was marshy and weedy, it teemed with natterjacks. I will own that till I came to Pinfold I wist not even that the natterjack existed. I had rolled him into one with his cousin the toad. But our only British brother, a leather-dresser from Bermondsey, and a born naturalist, soon showed me the difference. Ever since I have met the natterjack in society everywhere. He is the gentleman and the artist in his own family. Frogs croak, toads purr, but the natterjack sings. You will admire his clear high note, trilled with a delicate tremolo.

At last I fell asleep, a very wearied anarchist.

CHAPTER VII.

A MUTINOUS MUTINEER.

I RESPECTED Rothenburg; he was a man of ideas. Of course, they were wrong; but, according to his rush-lights, he acted them out. He seemed to me to have a shallow brain, in a constant state of feverish agitation. He was a flamboyant rhetorician, a crisp denunciator. It did one's soul good to hear him declaim redhot against kings, priests, and the intolerable tyranny of public opinion. The rest were shadows. Rothenburg by comparison was an intellectual Titan.

Even old Mrs. Pritchard, of the parboiled arms, who lived in the Community cottage with the bare, bald hall, recognised his superiority. "That there Rottenborough," she would say, with her arms akimbo, "why he's worth the whole lot of 'em." She was a study in her way, Mrs. Pritchard—globular and emotional. Rothenburg's eloquence filled her eyes with tears. *Why* she was an anarchist

I failed to perceive. She seemed as much out of place in that cosmopolite crew as a Free Kirk elder in a chorus of Mænads. She told me they had "convinced" her. If so, she must have had a mind singularly open to conviction. I gather rather that she took to anarchy as she might have taken to Primitive Methodism, the Salvation Army, or any other variety of dithyrambic religion. There chanced to be no Shakers or Mormons in the field at the moment, so Mrs. Pritchard fell back upon the allurements of Communism. She washed for the comrades, a post, you may guess, which almost amounted to a lady-like sinecure.

When I joined the Community I did so in dead earnest. You may think I jest, but I assure you seriously that my first intention was to live and die in the bosom of anarchy. Even the first sight of the ten acres, with its fringe of natterjacks and its total lack of eglantine, did not damp my ardour ; nor did the dinner at the outset. I reflected that I had taught a cookery class at the Guild, and that I could find an outlet for my energies in radical reform of the Communal kitchen. It certainly afforded a noble chance for the reformer. Meanwhile I said nothing, though I eat every

meal with an increasing undercurrent of distrust as to its cleanliness.

At night we gathered in the Community hall
and decided the future of Europe. Within, as
without, it had anæmic brick walls, slightly
inclined towards jaundice, and under its roof
we listened drearily while Rothenburg settled
the map of the twentieth century in unofficial
harangues. Save for his torrent of eloquence
I found the hall depressing. Our Community
shared the common mania of the sectary for
placarding its sentiments. Only here " The
Lord is my Shepherd " and " God Bless our
Home " gave place to " *Solidarité de la Race
Humaine*," " No King, no Laws, no Taxes,"
" *Das Land für das Volk*," " *Ubi bene, ibi
Patria*," and " Free Thought, Free Affection."
I read these legends over and over till they
palled. In another respect also my comrades
resembled the universal schismatic—their
interests were confined to a single range.
They were great on altruism ; but one saw
their eyes glaze over the moment one diverged
from the beaten path of anarchic platitude.

Rothenburg asked me the first day if I knew
anything of gardening. Anything of gardening ! I could have told them at a glance that
their cauliflowers were planted three inches

too close, while their views on spring carrots were absurdly elementary. I had been reared in the country. But I reflected that, even among anarchists, modesty befits a woman, and I answered that I hoped so.

They wished to set me at first upon light work in the glass-houses ; even those rough working men, I could see (notable mainly for the whiteness of their faces and the redness of their politics), paid some homage to my gentility ; though they would have denied it themselves, they were anxious to spare me as much as possible of manual labour. But I would have none of that. If I joined their clan at all I must join on equal terms. I am all for the absolute equation of the sexes. I wished to bear my part in the burdens of the Community.

So I devoted myself with a single mind to intensive culture. I may be dense, but after close inspection my impression is that intensive culture, were it not for its name, might readily be confused with ordinary gardening.

Rothenburg was working on the foundations of a new glass-house. To avoid Léon, whose province was potatoes, I took a pick and worked by the Alsatian's side. He seldom spoke ; when he did he left off delving

—his shallow brain had room but for one occupation at a time. It was curious to see him pause, push his crush-hat from his brow, wipe his narrow forehead with his shirt-sleeve, stroke the thin yellow hair, and then give vent to some deep philosophical speculation, which a child of ten might have considered profound.

On the second day of my task at the trench a sudden thought struck me. "Rothenburg," I said, wielding my pick somewhat viciously, "you have bought this land; how do you manage to hold it?"

He struck work, as usual, and turned the watery blue eyes upon me.

"We hold it, Juliet," he said—I was officially known to all the comrades as Juliet —"we hold it"—he paused as if I were drawing a tooth—"we hold it by trustees. No other way is possible."

"The English law compels you?"

"My faith, yes; we cannot own it as a Community."

" And suppose some comrade were to refuse to work, and yet stick to his rooms. What could you do to get rid of him?"

That was a problem for Rothenburg. He fondled the thin yellow hair till I thought it would come out; he fingered the shadowy moustache with that nervous hand till he made me frightened.

"I imagine," he said at last, after due deliberation, in a very slow tone, "we would be compelled to call in .   .   .   . the State .   .   .   . to eject him." He uttered that hated word with visible effort.

Appello Cæsarem! I dug my pick into the ground more viciously than ever. But I said nothing. Coercive practices! I saw I was back with my old friends Aforesaid and This Indenture Witnesseth.

Yet I will do the anarchists the justice to say that none of them seemed anxious to afford their pet bugbear, the State, the opportunity of trying this test case. They toiled hard, and inefficiently. In the sweat of their brow they did very little. None of them could be called a specialist in gardening. Rothenburg himself had worked as a lady's tailor in Paris, he told me, and had flung up a post of fifty francs a week—"Not bad wages for a working man," he observed, preening himself, with the complacency of a willing martyr—to till the soil with intensive culture. I believe he was really a good tailor spoiled to make an indifferent

F

gardener. Still, one could not help respecting his enthusiasm. When I pressed him further on this head, he admitted with regret that in the present state of the world only a chosen few—"like you and me, Juliet"— were fit for anarchy. (I felt half inclined to retort with the last of the Sandemanians, that I was "no that sure of Juliet.") However, he thought it was well to begin the experiment ; after all, one should live up to one's highest ideal.

I glanced around at the sodden field, the bald brick cottages, and had doubts in my mind whether they did really fulfil my highest ideal.

I worked hard with the rest. A certain sense of honour made me work my hardest. *Noblesse oblige ;* and precisely in proportion as I saw the comrades would be content to let me shirk some share of my task out of regard for my gentility, did I feel it incumbent upon me to do my utmost possible. I wore my cycling suit in the fields, and laboured like a man. I am not muscularly strong, but I have been well trained, and I honestly believe I was the most efficient workman in all that little group of incompetent town toilers.

In my spare time I set about reforming the kitchen. The vegetarian dishes I had learned at the Guild delighted the souls of the simple anarchists. My barley cutlets with tomato sauce were voted "heavenly" in best lip-licking Teutonic; my vermicelli shape received the praise of "bravissima" from our Neapolitan Luigi. This skill in cookery much increased my vogue among the men of the Community; while the women were not sorry to have their task lightened by a little amateur assistance.

If I have not said much here of the women and children 'tis not for want of appreciation: they were the salt of the settlement. There was no nonsense of high principles about them: they had followed their husbands and fathers and brothers to this outland spot as women will do; and they would have shouted "Vive l'Empereur" as heartily to-morrow as they shouted "Vive l'Anarchie" when asked to-day. But they loved to applaud Rothenburg on the war-path of peace, and would have scalped anyone who doubted the truth of the shibboleths of fraternity.

With the children I made great friends. Dear rough-and-tumble little things, they

F 2

oozed with merriment. My rational dress delighted them: so did Mr. Commissioner, with his white teeth, as soon as they had got over the first formalities. He suffered them to pull his tail like a lamb. We played games together at night, in the intervals of reorganising European affairs and abolishing the capitalist. We romped like tomboys. My attempts to tell them "Cinderella" and "The Three Bears," in bad German, translated by the more knowing into Czech and Yiddish, were not a complete success; but neither were they a failure, for at any rate they resulted in happy laughter. Besides I taught them cat's-cradle, and cat's-cradle at least has escaped the curse of Babel.

Still, rocks lay ahead. My Odyssey was not so quickly to bring me into port. By the end of the week a cloud took shape: I foresaw storms brewing.

All the comrades were devoted in equal parts to myself and my bicycle. In the evenings, when work was done, and we had watered the cabbages, I gave them lessons in turn on the mysterious monster. From the beginning it occurred to me that most of them were anxious to entice me away from the common field towards remoter lanes where occasions for private talk were more easily obtained. But, mindful of my promise not to form idolatrous attachments, I resisted the temptations of the polyglot Fausts who would fain have discoursed to me the words of love in many uncouth languages. It was my policy to keep close to the cottages and the other women, backed up by that round mountain of Britannic matronhood, the guile-less Mrs. Pritchard. Besides, in the Com-missioner, I had an efficient bodyguard.

On Saturday came the weekly division of profits. We had done well that week, having sent consignments of early roses and asparagus to Guildford and London. We declared a dividend, a splendid communal dividend, at the rate of four shillings per head for adults, and two shillings for children. I thought this profit magnificent. But just before the distribution of cash, Rothenburg strolled up to me, as I was dandling a mottle-armed anarchist. His fingers twitched on the imperceptible moustache more tremu-lously than ever. " Juliet," he said, briefly, " I want to speak to you."

He said it in the voice with which our Principal at College was wont to summon us to her study for the discipline of exhortation.

Free anarchist though I was, I listened and
trembled.

"Well, Rothenburg?" I murmured, laying
down the baby.

"The question is, do you mean to remain
with us?"

"Why, certainly," I cried, astonished.
"Did we not swear eternal friendship?"

"But—the comrades complain that you
take no notice of them."

"No notice! Absurd! Why, I have
taught them how to bicycle."

"Yes; but that is not everything. Friends
should show friendliness. You hold them at
arm's length. You keep yourself aloof. You
have no *camaraderie*."

I looked him hard in the face. He blinked
his watery eyes. I knew he was sincere—a
good, honest anarchist; but he expected too
much of me. "Rothenburg," I said firmly,
"I call this coercion."

"No, no; not coercion; but comrades
ought to be sociable."

"'Tis intolerable!" I exclaimed. "What
is anarchy for, if we are each to be forced
into talking to one another against our wills?
I have done my week's work; I have cooked you
good food; I have lent you my bicycle; and still

you complain of me. The Banded Despots"—
which was our technical phrase, to wit, for
the British Government—"could not do worse
than that, nor as bad as that either. They
do not insist that one should make oneself
agreeable. They are amply satisfied if man
pays man's taxes."

He twirled the non-existent moustache till
he put a visible point on it. His fingers
twitched painfully. "I only tell you what
the comrades are saying," he replied, in a
deprecatory way. "They find that you do
not behave to them like a sister. In one word,
they think that you give yourself the airs of
a superior person. You pose as an *aristo*.
They believed when you came that you would
amalgamate freely with us. We want no
women who decline to fraternise."

This was too much for my temper. I broke
into open mutiny. "I shall resign," I cried.
"You are bringing to bear against me the
intolerable tyranny of public opinion. I shall
go back to the freedom and comfort of the
Despots."

His jaw dropped at this resolve. His eye
glanced feelingly sideways towards the bicycle.
For a moment I feared Commissioner Lin
would pin him. "No, no," he cried. "You

must not do that. We all like and respect
you. We wish you to remain. But we wish
you to be a sister. Give me time to consider
—to communicate with the comrades."

" Not one moment," I answered, hardly
liking this turn. " Hand me over my money,
and let me go ! I have worked for a week,
and the labourer is worthy at least of his
travelling expenses. I return to London."

He hurried back to the group who hung
about the door of the Community cottage,
and spoke to them in low tones. Then he
came again as envoy. "All the comrades
say, if you will reconsider your decision, they
will no longer insist upon your altering your
demeanour."

" I will *not* reconsider it," I replied, growing really frightened, for I caught Léon's eye.
" I go at once. Give me my money, and let
me return to the world I came from."

They debated again. Commissioner Lin
watched the case in my interest. Then one
of the others approached. It was Léon—
Caliban—the man with the protruding lips.
I had my hand on my bicycle, and was ready
to mount it.

" This machine is ours," he said calmly,
putting his face close to mine. " Whatever

any comrade brings into the Community is common property. We will give you your dividend and let you go ; but this you must leave with us."

My blood was up. The old Eve within me was roused. The American eagle in my heart flapped its wings. I remembered how my fathers had fought at Lexington (they were quite a property to me). " Sir," I exclaimed, in my most commanding voice, "you shall not touch my machine. If you venture to detain it "—I tried to remember the worst phrases I had learnt at Flor and Fingelman's—"I will move for a mandamus to compel you to show cause why you should escape the penalties of præmunire." What it all meant I do not know ; but I am sure the effect upon Caliban's mind was most salutary. I have ever since had a vastly increased respect for the law of England.

They conferred again for a few minutes, with one eye on the Commissioner. Then Rothenburg came forward once more as spokesman. " Will you try it again for one week ? " he asked in a really grieved voice. " We shall be sorry to lose you."

" Not for one day !" I answered, a furtive gleam in Commissioner Lin's eye lending me

courage. "Give me what I have earned, and
let me go!" I asked for it with the greater
confidence because I felt sure in my own
mind I had done more effective work in the
week than any of them.

They paid me, murmuring. I retired to
my cubicle, packed my knapsack in haste,
returned to my machine, and laid my hand on
it firmly. But within I was trembling like
an Italian greyhound. Then I jumped into
the saddle, and waved my hand to my sworn
brothers, with an affectation of courage.
"Messieurs," I said—and to call them
"messieurs" was to excommunicate myself,
to deny *camaraderie*—"Messieurs, you are a
mass of conventions. I wish you the very
good morning. Your rules are too stringent
for me. I cannot away with them. I find
myself too individual, too anarchic for the
anarchists!"

Then I waved my hand again, and set my
face sternly towards civilisation, despotism,
and the flesh-pots of Egypt.

I was weary of dissent, and longed for the
catholic church of humanity. I must go back
to London, and be once more a type-writer.

CHAPTER VIII.

FOR the first three or four miles I kept on pedalling steadily. I grazed the corners, not even daring to look back, for I was haunted by a terror that Léon, with his lips, was on the track behind me. But I heard only the cries of the anarchist babies, calling to their playmate to come back in Czech and Yiddish.

When I had escaped from the intricate tangle of Sussex lanes, and found myself once more on the Queen's highway of England, under the protecting ægis of Britannia's shield (in spite of the blood of the Pilgrim Fathers), I paused to reflect upon the week's adventures.

A bicycle in full swing, I maintain, is not an ideal place for calm reflection. Hence the face of the bicyclist. Moreover, I had started without due attention to my screws, in my eagerness to escape from my sworn brothers, the anarchists, into the open air of Banded

Despotism. So I called a halt, and dismounted for a moment to tighten my loose
joints, metaphorically and literally. My
knees still trembled under me, and the
wraith of Caliban, panting ever in the
rear, still pursed its thick lips in my face
to mock me. I felt like Pliable when he
abandoned Christian at the outset of his
pilgrimage, and slank back from the first
slough to the City of Destruction. For, in
the background of my heart, I still loved
and admired these simple earnest souls,
eager after their kind to right human wrong,
and to attain human perfection. I saw their
comic side ; but I saw also that the root of
the matter was in them. They had noble
enthusiasms — all save Caliban ; he was
the serpent in that ten-acred Eden. When
I got under weigh again, at a good easy
pace, beneath rifts of blue through white
summer cloud, I began to be aware that my
first fortnight of free life had culminated
in two distinct and acknowledged failures.
I had failed to accommodate myself to the
environment at Flor and Fingelman's ; I had
failed to accommodate myself to the public
opinion of the anarchists at Pinfold. Environment was triumphing all along the line. I

ielt constrained to regard myself as one of the
unfittest, who do *not* survive, and whom no
man pities.

Resolving myself into Committee of Finance,
I found I had been acting with reckless extravagance. Cash in hand amounted to four
and sevenpence—of which sum, four shillings
represented my week's earnings, and sevenpence my balance from the bounty of St.
Nicholas, after settling for two weeks' rent
in London, with sundry expenses. It occurred
to me now (too late) that I had practically
been paying twice over for lodging—once in
London by cash, and once at the Community
by giving my labour in return for a mere box
of a cubicle. I felt so proud of this discovery
in economics, however, that I was almost inclined to condone the error for the sake of its
detection. In other ways, also, I was demon-
strably worse off than when I started. I had
worn my pretty brown cycling suit for a week
in the stiff clay fields, not to mention the fact
that I had splashed it with mud in the vica-
rious effort to rectify the lines of grace in
my comrades' riding ; and I had done my
tyres no good on the rough roads of Sussex.
Altogether, I was forced to confess to myself
with shame that I returned to London after

this escapade not only a wiser, but a poorer woman.

To crown all, I had no longer the use of my type-writer. The thirty pieces of silver for which I had betrayed my entire stock-in-trade, the instrument of production, were spent and lost to me. St. Nicholas had proved but a broken reed. I had leaned upon him, and he had pierced my hand. Never again should I trust the hypocritical smile on the face of that bland and benignant impostor !

I pedalled on at half-speed. Little vocalists, ignorant of the name of Mendelssohn, carolled songs without words in the sky overhead : but my heart was heavy.

Yet, after all, I had had my amusement, and bought my experience.

A pheasant screamed ; I mistook it for Caliban. Mr. Commissioner looked up in my face and sympathised.

It was still early afternoon ; for Saturday was a half-holiday : we had struck work at noon, and dined, before proceeding to the division of profits. June was almost come, and the days were lengthening. I hoped to reach London long before the hour at which the Banded Despots compel us to light our red lamps in the public interest.

Yet I was so delighted to have flung off
the yoke of anarchy that I could have fallen
on the neck of a Banded Despot, had he
appeared at that moment, were it but in the
guise of a Sussex County Constable. The
country smiled : if eglantine be sweet-briar, it
bordered the road; if honeysuckle, it scented
the cottage porches.

I rode on and on, glad to be free once more,
though sorry to be poor, and doubtful where
I could turn for the next few days' board and
lodging. The words of the anarchist alpha-
bet, which I had learned from the one British
brother at Pinfold, recurred strongly to my
mind—

> " F is the freedom that old England brags about ;
> If you haven't got a dinner—why—you're free to
> go without."

I felt sure I might soon taste that common
privilege secured to all of us by Magna
Charta.

In this mood I coasted recklessly down a
slight hill near Holmwood, with my feet on
the rest, and my hands too incautiously removed from the handle-bar. Behind me lay
the Weald ; in front rose the trenchant ram-
part of the North Downs.

At the foot of the slope was a sudden turn.

As I reached the bottom my hand gripped the break—too late. I was aware of a Foreign Body, rushing eagerly round the curve, with flying fair hair; next, of a considerable impact; then, of myself on the road, sprawling, and the Foreign Body with the fair hair wringing its hands beside me.

She was a woman, fortunately.

I raised myself with dignity. It is always a good plan, in case of collision, to take the aggressive first. "You came round that corner rather fast, considering how sharp it is," I observed in a coldly critical tone, whose effect was perhaps rather marred by the fact that my fingers were torn and bleeding. This was sheer bluff, and I knew it.

"Oh, I beg your pardon!" she cried, clapping her hands to her ears in an agonised little paroxysm. I saw that she was slight and fair and evidently frightened : a wisp of a figure, a fluff of amber hair, blue eyes like April.

"It was a nasty spill," I went on, growing severer in proportion as I realised that my antagonist was little inclined to defend herself (which was a meanness on my part). "You should slow round corners. I hope you have not hurt yourself."

She set to cry all at once. "A little," she answered. " Or rather, a great deal."

She was a timid small atomy. I began to regret my hasty sternness, the more so as I knew I was at least as much to blame as she, for I had run down the hill without my fingers on the break, and had trusted to chance at the turn of the corner. All this too, I admit, with a wheel that had already been badly buckled.

Happily, Commissioner Lin did not take it into his head to seize her.

I tried to console her. Then I turned to my machine. Which shows that I am a woman first and a cyclist afterwards ; for I notice that your born cyclist looks first at her wheels, and only proceeds in the second place to enquire which of her limbs is broken.

When I saw its condition, I recognised at once that my cup was full. All, all was lost. The front wheel was twisted out of human recognition ; the tyre was punctured ; I saw seven-and-sixpence worth of repairs staring me full in the face before I could fall back upon my base of operations in London.

I blush to confess it ; but I followed her example. Lexington faded away. I burst into tear. outright, and sank down on the

G

ground by my broken cycle. I suppose the
spill had shattered my nerves. Mr. Commissioner squatted on his haunches and stared
at me.

How long we might have sat there, ming-
ling tears together, it were hard to say—had
not St. George come by, in the nick of time,
sword in hand, to rescue us.

He was not mounted as usual on his milk-
white steed, but more prosaically seated on
the box of a dog-cart. Yet what matters
that? A cavalier is a cavalier, be he horseman
or gigman. The knights who ride in all
their pride around the frieze of the Parthenon are only knights in virtue of their pos-
session of the noble quadruped platonically
adored by the Grand Vizier and his satraps.
So I knew it was a St. George, though in
place of a lance he had a lancet in his instrument case. To unimaginative eyes he was
the village doctor.

He pulled up his horse by the roadside,
and called out to us cheerily : " Anything
wrong ? Can I be of use to you ? "

" Not for me," I broke out, fearing he
would want to dress my wounds and be
paid for it ; " I am not hurt at all. About
this lady I do not know. She cannoned

against me, and somebody seems to have
fallen."

St. George dismounted—if one can dis-
mount from a dog-cart—a genial giant. He
looked at my hands, which were torn and
bleeding, and ingrained with sand and dirt
from the road. "Excuse me," he said,
gravely ; "this is worse than you think.
You have had a nasty wrench. And, besides, the soil contains——"

" I know all that," I answered. " The
germs of lockjaw. I have gone through an
ambulance course, and helped the trained
nurse at an East-End Settlement. Well,
the germs must take their chance. Tetanus
microbes have a right to live like the rest of
us, I suppose."

My manner was perhaps defiant. He
smiled, not unkindly, a boundless Pacific of
a smile : his ears alone checked it. " Ha !
an anarchist ? " he enquired, glancing back
in the direction whence I had come.

" Yes," I answered. " From Pinfold."

" Tired of it ? "

" Very much so. I am on my way back to
London and the Banded Despots."

He smiled again. " You must let me
dress your hand," he said, persuasively.

G 2

I drew back in alarm. "Oh, no !" I cried, for I had nothing to pay him with.

"Nonsense," he went on with kind persistence, divining my thought in the hot flush that came over me. "This is not a professional matter. A mere passing courtesy to a lady in distress. Let me drive you to my surgery, and then on to Holmwood Station. You won't be able to get those machines mended so as to return to town to-night. I can pack them both in. And your friend will come with you."

There was no resisting the frank kindliness of his big genial smile. He was broad-shouldered and large-hearted, with a face to match. I clambered up into the dog-cart, and the fair girl sat behind. How he annihilated space so as to pack in the bicycles as well I have no idea. But the age of miracles is *not* past, nor yet the age of chivalry. St. George convinced me that both still exist. At a moment of despair, he revived my waning belief in human nature.

At the surgery, he washed my bleeding hands tenderly, spread an antiseptic ointment and a cool rag on top, and bound it all up with womanly solicitude. As a faint protest, I murmured at the end: "How much am I

in your debt ? "   But he smiled his expansive
smile, and repeated, "Nothing, nothing!"
Then he examined the fair girl, who was the
exact counterpart of Michaela in the opera,
and pronounced her sound in wind and
limb, though nervously shaken.   Michaela
wept at learning she was not hurt; she would
have fainted, I think, if he had told her she
was injured.

When our wounds had been assuaged, he
drove us down to the station.   On the way,
Michaela grew gradually calm enough to
communicate her misfortunes.   "I want to get
to Leith Hill," she said.   "I was going there
when I was so unlucky as to upset this lady."

(My heart pricked me, but I refrained from
confessing.)

"Leith Hill!" St. George cried, with his
hearty great laugh.   "Why, you are five
miles out for it !   You have taken the wrong
road.   You were straight on the way to
Horsham when I met you."

"Oh, I was afraid of that," Michaela exclaimed, beginning to cry again ; she had a
genius for tears that might have been utilised
with advantage for purposes of irrigation.
"I—I was cycling with a gentleman."

"Indeed ? " I put in coldly.

"But I—I am engaged to him."

"Of course," I answered. Having left anarchy and all its works nine miles behind me, I affected to believe *no* young lady could be bicycling with a man *unless* he were engaged to her.

"And we kept together as far as Dorking." Michaela went on; "but there I stopped to speak to some friends I met by chance in the street, and my—my escort went round the corner to buy some cigarettes; and when I hurried on again to catch him up, I could not discover him; and I'm afraid I must go back alone to London." She spoke as though London were in the heart of Africa.

The doctor laughed. "You took quite the wrong turn," he said. "Or rather, you kept straight on, when you should have swerved to the right. That unhappy young man must be seeking you now, on the summit of Leith Hill, with many qualms of conscience."

"Do you think so?" Michaela cried, wringing her hands once more. She was a study in helplessness. I could feel she was rich, brought up in cotton-wool, and for her sake I was glad of it; for I wondered what she would do if she should ever find herself face to face with real misfortune.

CHAPTER IX.

I PLAY CARMEN.

St. George joined tact to his chivalry. When we pulled up at the station, he handed us both out, unloaded our iron steeds, raised his hat with an amicable smile, and then, before we had time to thank him, cracked a merry whip, and drove away hurriedly. My bandaged condition forbade me even to grasp his hand ; he vanished into the past, and was once more a phantom. I never saw him again. Yet I have always been grateful to that brief vision of a knight who saved me for one moment from a passing dragon. If peradventure he happen to read these words, will he accept my thanks for it ?

On the platform, as Chancellor of my own Exchequer, I had time to bring in my private budget. It showed an obvious deficit. Had I been Leader of the Opposition, I could have risen with scorn from the front bench, and subjected it to a scathing—nay, a crushing criticism. In plain words, I saw that I had not money enough to pay my way back to London, to take a dog-ticket for the Commissioner, and also to carry my bicycle with me (zone 50, one shilling.) This collision had proved even more disastrous to my finances than to my hands. Two courses were now open to me. I must cloak-room my machine—with little chance of redeeming it—or else resolve to spend the residue of my days at Holmwood.

The latter alternative being the more original of the two, naturally I made up my mind to adopt it. I felt so poor and desolate that I looked for the police to step in and disperse me.

"I won't go up to town," I said curtly to Michaela. "I will spend the night here." I said "the night" only, instead of "my life," lest she should suspect me of exaggeration.

To my vast surprise, this resolution, which I fancied of no importance to anyone save myself, threw my companion into a tremor of anxiety. "Then I can't go either," she cried, wetting her lips with fear. "If *you* stop, *I* must stop with you, and telegraph up for my father."

I stared at her in astonishment. "Why so?" I asked at last.

"Why, because—because of this *dreadful* murder!"

"What murder?" I inquired, reverting instinctively to Léon and his lips.

She stared in turn. "You *must* have heard of it," she exclaimed. "It has been in all the papers."

I remembered that at Pinfold we had been too much absorbed by the future of Europe and the affair of the new glass-house ever to trouble our minds about what chanced to be happening in the mere provincial world of London. So I assured her I knew naught of it.

She went on to explain to me that a woman had been found killed in a first-class carriage —stabbed to the heart, and stuffed under the seat—only three days before.

"I *dare* not travel alone," she said, clasping her hands and opening her blue eyes wide. "Do *please* come with me."

This forced me to explain my financial position. My new friend declared that that did not matter. Might she lend me a sovereign? A sovereign! I gasped at the idea of such wealth. But I had further to make it clear that my chance of repaying it was a vanishing quantity.

She listened to my explanation with open-mouthed astonishment. I think she had never heard of such poverty before—in one of her own sort—though to me it was commonplace. "But you *must* let me lend it to you," she said, drawing out the daintiest little lizard-skin purse I have ever seen ; "or, rather, you must let me pay you for the harm I have done to your bicycle, and the difficulty I have brought upon you. That is only fair. I ought to settle for your ticket up to town, and for the mending."

I was compelled to confess. My duplicity had failed. "It was more my fault than yours," I faltered out. "I was reckless in my pace. You were mounting a slight rise, with the wind against you : I was descending, and had it in my favour. If anybody is to blame, it is I. Pray, pray, forgive me."

She insisted in spite of me. "I shall take two first-class tickets."

My democratic gorge rose. "Never!" I cried firmly. "St. Nicholas forfend! Not in my palmiest and most unregenerate days did I travel first-class. If you consent to take two thirds, I will owe you for the amount. You can give me your address ; and whenever I am rich enough I will repay you all. I have sufficient of my own to buy a ticket for my dog and bicycle." It went against the grain with me to receive this favour from a stranger unseen till to-day ; but I recognised that there was no help for it.

She took the tickets under protest. " Such *dreadful* people travel third—drunken soldiers and sailors ! "

"Brave defenders of our country ! " I answered, remembering my father's profession. " It's *Thank you, Mr. Atkins*, when the band begins to play."

The liquid blue eyes stared at me in blank amazement. Rudyard Kipling, one could see, was a sealed book to her. I think she had doubts of my perfect sanity. Perhaps you share them.

We arranged for our maimed mounts. I hold it one of the best points of a bicycle, as compared with the noble animal, that it considerately refrains from wringing your heart in the matter of sympathy. It has no nerves. The train panted into the station. We explored an empty carriage, free from the contamination of soldiers and sailors, drunk or sober, and started off comfortably.

Michaela took the precaution to peer under the seats beforehand. I am not sure which of the two she expected to find—a corpse or a murderer.

"This is nice," she said at last, smiling, and recovering her spirits for the first time since the collision. "We shall have the carriage to ourselves all the way to Victoria. I gave the guard half-a-crown. I *couldn't* travel with a man. I should be quite too frightened."

Some devil entered into me. I am subject to devils. My new acquaintance was so insipidly fair, so mediævally shrinking, while I am dark and modern, that I had an irresistible impulse to play Carmen to her Michaela. "Have you reflected," I said drily, "that a *woman* may have committed that murder?"

It was heartless of me, I admit. My little companion was so timid and shrinking. But the bolt fell flat. She clasped her hands and looked at me. "I never thought of that!" she said. "How *dreadfully* clever you must be to discover it. Dreadful as well as clever! But I am *sure* you are not a murderess." (She had a trick of emphasising one word in each sentence.) "You are a *great* deal too nice.

You behaved so sweetly about the ticket, you know, and the accident! Anyone else in your place would have pretended it was my fault, and made me pay for the damages."

"That was only common honesty," I objected. "Murderers need not be deficient in common honesty."

"Oh, but they must be awful people!"

"Murderers are not a class," said I. "They are you and me, acting under pressure of powerful impulses."

She glanced at me, more amazed than frightened. "I *know* you would not murder me," she replied, less alarmed than I might have expected. "You are so kind, though you are so queer. I feel quite safe in your hands. With those honest eyes I am certain you would not hurt me."

I could have crept under the seat, I felt such a brute. I took her two small hands in my bandaged palms. "You dear little thing!" I exclaimed, "nobody could ever hurt you!" Then seven other devils entered into me again, worse than the first ones, and I could not help adding, "Though if I *wanted* to murder, this is a unique opportunity. My bleeding hands, and the evidence about the bicycle accident would suffice to account for any number of

blood-stains. Still, to stuff you under the seat
would be bad taste and vulgar."

She caught my eye, and laughed. " What
a funny girl it is ! " she cried. " You *are* so
comical ! But it isn't the least use your trying
to frighten me. I can see the twinkle in your
big black eyes ; and I like you in spite of your
trying to be horrid. Do you know, I liked
you from the first moment I saw you."

'Twas impossible not to be taken by such
charming childishness. She cooed so pret-
tily one was forced to love her. Before we
reached Victoria we were fast friends. Michaela
thought me the queerest person she had ever
met, but, oh, so nice ! Her tongue was
loosed. She told me a great deal about what
a dear fellow she was engaged to. She spoke
of him as Toto. She also wanted to lend me
a pound. But I sternly refused. I must work
out my own salvation in fear and trembling.
(This Biblical trick descends to me, no doubt,
from the Pilgrim Fathers.)

Michaela gave me her card at Clapham
Junction — "Miss Allardyce" it said — and
begged me to call upon her. I was driven
to explain that in the rank of life to which
I now belonged people did not call upon one
another; more particularly that the Jews of

Onslow Gardens (I am dropping into it again) had no dealings with the Soho Samaritans. Michaela dissented from this finding : her position was that " a lady was a lady." I granted the truth of that identical proposition, but flatly disallowed that all ladies had time for calling. I also pointed out that my first consideration was bread, which brought tears again into her tender blue eyes. We parted the best of friends. We even kissed one another, though I am an infrequent kisser. She thanked me mightily for my company, which made me feel small again. For I had upset her nerves, broken her machine, and borrowed some shillings, which I scarcely dared to hope I might have the luck to repay her.

However, I took her address, and added one small square to the mosaic design with which I am paving my possible future residence.

CHAPTER X.

SIC ME SERVAVIT APOLLO !

PERHAPS you think I have made too much of those ancestors of mine who fought and bled at Lexington. That is always possible; if so, on further thought, you will feel that there are excuses for me. My ancestors bequeathed me nothing save the memory of their courage. Had I inherited from them an estate in Middlesex, or even in Massachusetts, I might dwell less on their valour. But since they have left me heiress of their glory alone, 'tis natural that I should magnify the one legacy I have received from them. To deprive me of that pittance were to leave me poor indeed. Let me salve my indigence with the honour of the family.

And, in truth, when I got back to my rooms in Soho, I stood in need of every ghost among my ancestral warriors. All the dragons in London flapped wings together in that narrow lodging.

Picture my position. I had no money in hand, and no machine to work upon. Besides, with my maimed fingers, it would be impossible for me to type-write for three days at least. I had no prospect of food till my wounds recovered. Even then, much must depend upon the chance of an engagement; and for record of my " last place " what had I but my mocking letter to This Indenture Witnesseth ?

Must I fall back on the aunt, with her black thread gloves and her Zenana Missions ? I glanced at Commissioner Lin ; no, a bone, and freedom !

However, petty troubles are the mustard of life: they add pungency. Besides, we are all Cinderellas with a fairy godmother. Her name is Aide-toi-et-Dieu-t'aidera. I have never failed to find much efficacy in Citizen Danton's prescription. In hopeless circumstances our three best allies are audacity, audacity, and again audacity.

I made up my mind to be audacious. I have big black eyes, as Michaela had truly observed, so audacity comes easily to me ; celestial blue is always shrinking. I presented myself at the door of my lodgings with the air of one who had merely gone away for a few

H

days' bicycling trip, and had thousands at her banker's. I think my jauntiness impressed the landlady. I spoke in vague terms of "a tour in Sussex," and of its premature close through the accident of a collision. Item, the knees of my knickerbockers had distinctly suffered. However, as I had paid a fortnight's rent before I left, out of St. Nicholas's benefaction, and had been away for a week and a day, besides four days more or less spent at Flor and Fingelman's, I was still entitled to two clear nights' lodging. If the worst came, I might even stop on for another week without paying. The mere fact of my return was a guarantee of "respectability," which, in the lodging-house acceptation, is a synonym for probable continuous solvency.

I commanded supper with my lordliest air. My landlady was too much taken aback to refuse me. I suggested a chop, as though chops grew wild. She acquiesced without a murmur.

I have remarked already that I belong to a generation which has analysed conscience away. But I am sorry to say analysis is not really one with annihilation. Conscience resembles nature in that, when driven out with a pitchfork, it recurs in spite of you. My enjoyment of that excellent chump chop—grilled brown to a turn—was sadly interfered with by the floating fear that I might never be able to pay for it. I had painful qualms. Had my landlady been rich, I might have swallowed them with the chop : but she was a reduced widow with one invalid daughter.

Conscience, however, though it makes cowards of us all, does not (within my experience) produce insomnia. I slept the sleep of the just, and woke up an Antæus, or rather an Antæa. (This remark I offer as a contribution to the unsolved problem whether or not I have been to Girton.)

The sun was shining. The thrushes (at the bird fancier's opposite) were bent on justifying Browning, by singing twice over each careless *leit-motiv*. I ordered breakfast with an undaunted face, like Leonidas at Thermopylæ. The landlady, completely subdued, brought up coffee and rolls as if I had been a duchess. I almost soared to an egg ; as the word hung on my lips, conscience stepped in with " Necessaries, yes ; but luxuries—that were an infamy." I forewent the egg, though my long ride had begotten in me a noble hunger. And I rather flatter myself that in saying " forewent " I am en-

riching the language with a new preterite.
Oxford Dictionary, please copy.

Breakfast inspired me with fresh hope.
There is much virtue in a breakfast. I began
to surmise that I might have misjudged St.
Nicholas. Not the bland old bishop of the
National Gallery—he was a humbug, I felt
sure—but that charming young benefactor
in Fra Angelico's panel ; could he be equally
untrustworthy, and with so innocent a face ?
I, for one, could scarce credit it. He
seemed like the masculine counterpart of
Michaela. And Michaela was too mild not
to be really guileless.

At least, I would stroll round to the Strand
and seek another interview with the holy
man. For the next two days it were futile
to hunt for work. Those bandaged hands
must tell against me. So perforce I took
holiday.

On Monday morning I sallied forth. I
wore my little black dress and hat, in which,
even to myself, I looked absurdly proper.
I love trudging down the Strand. It may
sound ungrateful to confess it, after the pains
that have been taken to make London ugly
for us, but I find a weird charm in its pic-
turesque ugliness. When I reached the win-

dow of which I was in search, a sudden thrill ran through me.   It seemed as though I had suffered some personal loss.   My patron saint had disappeared!   Not a trace of St. Nicholas!

If the embalmed body of the holy bishop had been missing from the shrine where it lies at Bari, still exuding manna, I could not have been more disconcerted.   In my surprise and alarm I even ventured into the shop.   "The little Fra Angelico," I cried, " in the window—what has become of it ? "

My anxious manner made the astute proprietor scent a possible purchaser.   " Put up to auction to-day," he answered.   " You must be quick if you want it."

" Where ? "

He mentioned a firm of picture-dealers in the West-End.

I know not what possessed me—unless it were the fairy godmother—but I hurried off to the sale-rooms.   I had never attended an auction before, yet I wedged my way to the front with the assured air of a buyer.

I was only just in time.   My patron saint was in the hands of the slave-dealer, who expatiated, after the usual fashion of slave-dealers, on his chattel's youth, simplicity,

and beauty. He also called attention to the
innocence and charm of the three sleeping
maidens. His language was florid. I could
not help wondering whether, from some calm
cell in the heavenly monastery overhead, the
angelic friar looked down with a pitying
smile on this vicissitude of his handicraft.
How lovingly he laid on his cinnabar and his
cobalt ! He painted that picture with holy
joy for some dim niche in a Florentine
nunnery ; could he have foreseen how it
would be bandied about, with unsympathetic
remarks as to its drawing and colouring,
in the unsanctified hands of far northern
heretics ?

It was hateful to behold that lovely youth,
with his long fair hair and his delicate trunk-
hose, held up for competition to the highest
bidder. The desecration sickened me. There
he stood on tip-toe, his back half-turned to
us, with his three purses of gold, a rich and
noble saint, yet not wealthy enough to redeem himself from such last dishonour ! Oh,
strange craft of the brush which could so give
life to a dead thing that, ages after its
fashioner had mouldered into dust, my heart
still went forth to it as to a living lover !
Men began to bid for St. Nicholas. Thirty,

forty, fifty, sixty guineas; seventy guineas
for the saint ; slower, slower, slower.

At last the auctioneer reached a hundred.
Then came a long pause. I could not bear to
think that that coarse-looking dealer with the
vulgar laugh—fat, sleek, materialised—should
possess my patron. A young man with a
sweet voice (on whose forehead I seemed to
see the red star of St. Dominic) had bid up to
ninety-five. How I hoped he would continue! But he was silent at the hundred. I
could no longer contain myself. The fairy
godmother at my elbow impelled me. With
an effort I gasped out, "A hundred and
five!"—just to keep up the bidding.

"Going at a hundred and five! A hundred
and five guineas! A genuine Fra Angelico!
This exquisite work! *So* small a price!
Does no other gentleman offer?" He made
a dramatic pause. Then down came the
hammer. "The lady has it."

In a second it rushed over me what I had
done. I gasped in my embarrassment. A
clerk drew near and murmured something
inaudible about "conditions of sale." Through
a mist of words I caught faint echoes of
"Five per cent. at once, and the balance
before to-morrow."

My face was fiery red. I had dim dreams of prison. The young man with the sweet voice stole quietly up to me.

"Excuse me," he said, in my ear; "one moment, before you complete this purchase. I want that picture. *Will* you take five guineas for your bargain?"

"Five guineas?" I cried, aghast. "For a picture worth more than a hundred."

"You misunderstand me," he corrected. "I want that work very much—though I doubt its authenticity: I believe it to be only a contemporary replica. However, if you cede it to me, I will pay the money down and give you five guineas over. I did not care to go on bidding further against the dealer; he was running up the price: but I will buy it from *you*. Do you accept my offer?"

Sic me servavit Apollo! Thus St. Nicholas saved me! I repented of my distrust, Twice was he tried at a pinch, and twice not found wanting!

In a haze, I assented. The stranger paid me the money, which I handed over to the clerk, less my own profit. Then I went forth into the street, a rich woman once more, with an almost inexhaustible capital of five guineas.

Was it St. Nicholas, I wonder, or the fairy godmother ?

The question is important, from the doctrinal point of view, for it involves the conflict between the faith and paganism.

But my own opinion is that the young man with the star of Dominic on his brow was St. Nicholas himself, come down to earth yet another time with a purse of five guineas for a maiden's dower. So have I seen him more than once descending from solid clouds, in *ex voto's* in Italy.

CHAPTER XI.

A SAIL ON THE HORIZON.

" This story," you say, "is deficient in love-interest."

My dear critic, has anybody more reason to regret that fact than its author? I have felt it all along. Yet reflect upon the circumstances. Ten thousand type-writer girls crowd London to-day, and 'tis precisely in this that their life is deficient—love-interest.

Remember, I am only telling you my own poor little story; and I am but an amateur story-teller. The professional novelist keeps in stock in her study a large number of vats, each marked (like drinks in a refreshment-room) with the names of their contents in gilt letters—" Sensation," " Character-sketches," " Humour," and so forth. She turns on the taps mechanically as they are needed. But by far the biggest vat is labelled " Love-interest." No matter what plot the professional novelist may invent, she lets this tap run, as soon as her puppets are devised, and drenches the whole work with an amatory solvent, exactly as the chemist dilutes his mixtures with distilled water to eight ounces. I, however, who am narrating to you the actual history of one stray girl among ten thousand in London,—what can I do but wait for the love-interest to develop itself?

My name is Juliet; you may well believe I have had moments when I thrilled with the expectation of a Romeo. But Romeos do not grow on every gooseberry bush. It were unreasonable to expect that any mere man is sufficient. You will admit, for instance, that neither the Grand Vizier, nor Rothenburg of the watery eyes, was precisely the ideal knight my fancy painted. St. George, to be sure, was a dear: but I suspected him of one fatal flaw—being married.

I waited and watched for that not impossible he; and the not impossible he still lurked unmaterialised.

When I came into my fortune (of five guineas) my first impulse was naturally to repay Michaela (which I did at once by post-office order), and thus to transfer that particular square of mosaic pavement from its nether abode to some celestial mansion. My second

was, to buy a bunch of tea-roses for my
lodgings : and my third, to redeem my type-
writer, so as to return to St. Nicholas, as
some small mark of my gratitude, thirty
shillings from his latest benefaction.

On further thought, however, it occurred
to me that thirty shillings in the hand are
worth more at a crisis than a type-writer in
the bush—a mixed metaphor which not even
the printer's reader with his officious query
shall prevail upon me to rectify. If no work
came, I could live upon capital once more.
Meanwhile, the machine could be of no possible service.

After three days, my hands were so far recovered that I began to look about me for a
situation again. I took up a daily paper and,
in a column of mixed wants, read another
"Wanted" advertisement: "Lady type-writer,
with good knowledge of shorthand. Apply,
Messrs. Blank and Sons, Publishers,"—and
the address followed.

I liked the idea of a publisher's office, and
I liked that advertisement. My theory is that
a type-writer girl should call herself a type-
writer girl ; but that an advertiser should do
her the courtesy to speak of her as a Lady
Type-writer, or something of the sort : cer-

tainly not as a (parenthetical) female. Also, I must have literature. The literature at my aunt's consisted of ladies' newspapers, Bishop Jackson on "The Sinfulness of Little Sins," and books about the Holy Land. Here, I should have access to the Springs of Culture.

So I hastened to apply for the vacant post. I was not the first this time; I met a girl on the stairs, less strong than myself, coming down from the office with a most dejected countenance. If this were the struggle for life, it made my heart ache (for her sake) to think I must engage in it. However, I continued on my way, and boldly stated my errand to the young man in attendance. That young man struck a keynote. He was neat, well-dressed, and had a black fringe of moustache; in spite of which advantages he was not supercilious. His voice was a gentleman's. He told me Mr. Blank would be disengaged in a moment; meanwhile, would I take a seat? I sank into one and waited.

The office was quite unlike Messrs. Flor and Fingelman's. The anteroom where I sat was exquisitely clean, and neatly fitted up with polished shelves and wood-work. An air of quiet culture pervaded the whole; it seemed to communicate itself even to the clerks. In the pigeon-holes round the room stood rows of books in glazed paper covers, looking as spotless and as tidy as if a woman had arranged them. Well-known names adorned their backs. As for dust, it was not.

In a few minutes came the word, " Mr. Blank will see you."

I followed my guide, expecting to be ushered into a rather bare room with a venerable gentleman seated at a table ; I pictured him, in fact, as the exact original of the hale old grey-beard who testifies in the omnibuses to the merits of Eno's Fruit Salt. For the firm is one of the most dignified in London. Instead of that, I found myself in a neat study, —too cosy for an office, too severe for a boudoir. It had curtains of silken Samarcand, and fittings of cedared Lebanon. It had also a tawny Oriental carpet, and an old oak desk, at which sat a young man of modest and statuesque countenance. I guessed his age at twenty-seven. He rose undecided as I entered, like one whom native politeness impels to an act which he half fears is ill-suited to the occasion. As he turned towards me, I saw a face of notable strength and culture ; a finely-modelled nose, firm, yet soft in out-

line ; acute brown eyes, piercing, but gentle ;
abundant dark eyebrows that hung slightly
over them and gave a masterful air to their
keenness and penetration. His hair was
black and shaggy, like a retriever's. He was
tall, but well-knit. His eyes met mine as he
gave a little inclination. A thrill ran through
me. I knew him as by instinct. I said to
myself, " A Romeo ! "

I suppose I was the only person in London
at the time who did not know that the head
of the firm had lately died, and been succeeded by his son, an Eton boy and Oxford
man, who had taken high honours.

Romeo waved me to a chair. " You have
come, I think," he said, in a rich, clear voice,
pausing for a minute out of instinctive courtesy before he seated himself, " in answer to
our advertisement."

" Yes," I replied ; " I understand you want
a type-writer girl."

His eyebrows moved up at the words. I
could see they produced a favourable impression. He was accustomed to the formula
" a lady to type-write for you."

" Exactly," he answered, folding his hands,
and trying to assume the official tone of a man
of business ; though I was aware that he

was unobtrusively observing my dress and appearance, not as Ahasuerus had done, like a cross between an Oriental monarch and a horse-dealer, but like a gentleman of keen insight, accustomed to take things in at a glance without disconcerting the object of his scrutiny.

He put me a few stereotyped questions as to speed and qualifications, which I was fortunately able to answer to his satisfaction. Then he went on in a deprecatory way, " I must ask you, I am afraid, to w. .e a little to my dictation, and then transcribe what you have written. Excuse this detail. One must test your ability."

" Of course," I assented, producing my stylograph.

" We have had applicants already who did not suit my requirements. One left as you arrived. I—I was sorry not to be able to engage her ; for I judged her to be in want ; but—she was quite incompetent." He spoke apologetically.

" I met her on the stairs," I replied. " She appeared to be downcast."

He gave me a hurried glance, for there was pity in my tone. "It is *so* unfortunate," he said, "that one must insist on competence !

For often the incompetent most need employment."

"There is a beautiful story," I answered,
"about Robert Owen, when somebody patted
the head of a very pretty child at his school
at Harmony Hall. 'You are like all the rest,'
said Owen; 'you pat the prettiest. But it
is the ugly ones that need encouragement.'
That was true philanthropy."

He looked me through and through. I
took out my note-book, and assumed a busi-
ness-like air. He reached down a volume of
some History of Greece, and began dictating
rapidly. The passage, chosen of set purpose,
was full of Greek names, and rather recondite
words of technical import. I saw he had
selected it as a test of knowledge as well as
of speed. I was glad I had been at——But
that would be confessing. I wrote rapidly
and well—more rapidly, I think, than I had
ever before done ; and I knew why : he was
a Romeo.

"Do I go too fast ? " he asked at last,
looking up at me suddenly with a gentle
smile.

"Not at all," I replied. "You might try a
little faster, if you like, as you really wish to
test me."

I

"And you know the names?" he inquired with an incredulous accent.

"Perfectly. Please go on; 'the hegemony of Thebes' was the last clause you dictated."

He continued to the end. 'Bœotia thus lost the flower of her hoplites,' were the words with which he finished.

I wrote it all out in long-hand, very clearly and distinctly. He ran his eye over it. "But this is excellent!" he said at last, glancing at it close. "You have all the words right. You must have studied Greek, haven't you?"

I temporised. "A little."

He paused again. Then, after a few questions to draw me out, especially as to attainments, he began rather timidly. "This is precisely what I want. I require a lady of education, who can take down instructions and write letters to authors on the subject-matter of their works, without need for correction. But—I'm afraid the post would hardly suit you. If you will excuse my saying so, you are too good for the place. I do not mean as to salary—that, no doubt, I could arrange . . . in accordance . . . with qualifications." He glanced quickly at my black dress again. "But I fear—I fear you will find the work beneath you."

"You can set your mind entirely at rest on that score,' I answered frankly. "I will tell you the plain truth—I am in need of a situation, and shall be glad to get one."

He hesitated once more. "Still, I feel doubts of conscience," he went on. "I will be quite open with you. You may think me quixotic, but I have ideas of my own—social ideas—some people might even say socialistic. Here is this work, which I have it in my hands to bestow; which I hold as a trust, almost. It would suffice to keep some poor lady's wants supplied—some lady who is in need of actual necessaries. Now, I do not think it right that young gentlewomen who have all they need already found them at home should compete in the market against poor girls in search of a bare subsistence. They ought not to deprive such girls of bread in order to add to their own pin-money. This movement for 'doing something' on the part of well-to-do women is pressing hard on the girls of the lower middle-class. Pardon my putting it so ; but you come from a home, no doubt, where you have all you require ; and you seek this work just to increase your income."

I thought it was sweet of him. I could see I was exactly the person he wanted ; yet for a matter of principle he was prepared to take someone possibly less suited to his special requirements. I was glad that I could answer with the ring of truth, "There, you are quite mistaken. I am one of the class whom you desire to employ—in fact, a girl in search of a bare subsistence. I do not say so in order to appeal to your generosity ; I only wish to obtain work on my merits for what my services are worth in the open market But if, as you say, I prove a suitable person for your purpose in other respects, you need have no scruple on the grounds you suggest about employing me. I have nothing to live upon save what I can earn by type-writing."

He blushed like a girl of eighteen. He was distressed that he had driven me into making this avowal. "Oh, forgive me," he said, rising again from his chair. "I—it was awkward of me to put it thus bluntly. But you are so evidently a lady of education that I took it for granted—you will understand my natural error. I only hesitated to give a post which might be filled by a person in need of employment to an amateur who wanted occupation and pocket-money."

"I quite understand," I answered. "Out bicycling last week, I passed a common where shaggy donkeys, with unkempt coats, stood in the sunshine dejected, hanging their heads as if they had been reading Schopenhauer." (He looked up suddenly at the name with an inquiring glance.) "But their mood was justified; for geese were tugging at the short grass hard by, nibbling it close to the root; and I felt the four-footed beasts might well be melancholy at the struggle for life when birds, winged creatures that may career over the world, took to competing with them by grazing like cattle, and snatched the bread out of the donkey's mouth."

His face wore an amused smile. "But you are learned," he put in. "You might obviously be engaged in so much higher work—a teacher's, for instance."

"I should hate teaching!" I cried vehemently. "I prefer freedom. I am prepared for the drudgery of earning my livelihood in a house of business. But I must realise myself."

"I understand that," he answered; "and—and sympathise with it. Well, I apologise for my mistake. Under the circumstances, we need only proceed to arrange the business part of this transaction."

He named a weekly sum. It was my turn to blush. "That is too much," I exclaimed. I could see he was fixing it, not by the market price, but by what he thought a sufficient income for a person of my presumed position in society. It was all so alien from Ahasuerus's way of hiring a Shorthand and Type-writer (female).

"Not for so competent an assistant," he answered, still nervous.

Awkward as it might be to begin one's relations with a new employer by an apparent contest of generosity, yet I could not accept the sum he proposed. I told him so in plain words: he insisted: I beat him down. After a brief but well-contested skirmish, I camped on the field as victor, though we compromised for a wage a little less than half-way between what he wished to give and what I was prepared to accept. It did not escape me at the time, however, that such a first step almost of necessity entailed a certain sentimental tinge in our relations: they would scarce be those of employer and employed, as regulated by custom and political economy.

When all protocols were settled he went on, "Can you come in at once?"

"To-day, if you wish it."

"Oh, that would be such a convenience to me! I have matters to settle which I do not wish to hand over just now to my clerks; it was my desire that you should act as confidential letter-writer in my dealings with authors, quite outside the business."

"I will begin this afternoon," I said.

"Our type-writing machine—the one I intended for you—is——." I forget precisely which make he mentioned, but it was one to whose keyboard I was unaccustomed. "Can you work with it?"

"No," I answered. "But I have my own. I will bring it."

"How kind of you! Though you must not continue to use it, of course. We have no right to impose upon you the wear and tear. If you will tell me which sort you prefer, it shall be here to-morrow. Meanwhile, for to-day, if you would bring round your own, I should be greatly obliged to you."

"I will go and fetch it," I said, remembering that it lay close by in St. Nicholas's safe keeping.

"How? In a cab?"

I smiled. His politeness positively embarrassed me. "No; in my hands," I replied. "I am accustomed to carry it."

"But type-writers are so heavy," he remonstrated. (I felt his anxiety to treat me like a lady was leading to complications, and I half regretted the Grand Vizier's lofty sense of masculine superiority.) " Had you not better take a cab ? "

"No," I answered with firmness ; for I felt I must put a stop to this strain at the outset. An employer should know his place. " I can carry it easily, thank you."

He looked at me with a curious look. I suppose I have the average endowment of feminine intuition; and I felt sure he was debating in his own mind whether or not he should tell me to call a hansom and charge it to the office. It was my own old duologue of Inclination and Duty. Inclination said, " Make her take it "; Duty interposed, " You must begin as you mean to go on. This is an office matter. If she cannot work your machine, and wishes to bring her own, she must convey it at her own expense. You have no ground to stand upon."

After a pause in which, as I could see, either impulse got the upper hand alternately, he compromised the matter. " Is it far ? " he enquired.

"Close by. I can fetch it in five minutes."

"Then one of my clerks will step round with you and carry it for you."

I blushed bright crimson. I had imagined shyness to be (like "sensibility," hysterics, and fainting) an obsolete disease of the early Victorian epoch. I now knew that it survived into our own time. I could feel the hot blood flooding my ears and cheeks, and running down my neck. What on earth could I answer? How let the clerk see where I had left my machine? How confess to Romeo to whose keeping I had confided it? He could never understand that, to a girl of my temperament, those golden balls were but the mystic symbol of the saint of Myra. I knew not what to answer. I stood still and blushed; and my blush it was that betrayed, yet saved me.

Lifting my eyes one second in a mute appeal, I saw right into his soul as he stood there, facing me, more nervous, more embarrassed than ever. I saw he divined that I lived in some poor quarter, or had a drunken mother, or something equally discreditable, and was ashamed to let his clerk know it. But he withdrew, like a gentleman that he was to the finger-ends. "How stupid of me!" he went on. "I see, of course, it would

be unpleasant for you to walk down the
street with one of my clerks—though they
are nice young men, all of them.   Excuse my
gaucherie.   But—you are coming in at once
to oblige me ; I ought to have arranged to
have a machine here to suit you.   Won't you
please take a cab, and allow me to—to charge
it to the office ?"

He had got it out at last.   I changed colour
once more.   To hide my shyness—for to my
vast surprise, I was speechlessly shy by this
time—I pulled out my handkerchief.   As fate
would have it—fate that mocks at human
souls—I drew with it from my pocket a little
square of blue paper which fell, face downward, on the floor.   How can I confess the
truth ?   It was—the counterfoil or ticket I
had received for my machine from the repre-
sentative of St. Nicholas.

CHAPTER XII.

A CAVALIER MAKES ADVANCES.

I GRIEVE to hint a doubt of my chosen patron, but enlarged experience of St. Nicholas has led me to believe that he lacks consistency. His action is jerky. Though he will often sweep down, as of old, in a pale haze of glory, to rescue some votary from instant shipwreck, he is hardly a saint in whom a girl can repose implicit confidence. At tight places of social trial he is apt to fail one.

I had but one consolation. The ticket had fallen on the floor face downward.

I stooped to pick it up. My cheeks, I feel sure, must have glowed with crimson. Shame tingled in my ears. But Romeo was beforehand with me. He raised the scrap of paper and handed it to me, still face downward, with a faint inclination. I lifted my lowered eyelids. My swimming eyes parleyed with his for a second. I cannot say whether he was aware what manner of thing

he was passing me ; but I fancy he *did* know.
Yet if he knew I felt sure he interpreted the
episode aright, for his glance was one of mute
respect and sympathy.

I crushed the unspeakable pasteboard into
my pocket, never uttering a word, and rushed,
hot and red, from the room, without daring to
speak to him.

On the stairs I debated whether I could
ever come back. Prudence and Shame fought
it out between them. Prudence won. I determined to go on as if nought untoward had
happened.

I might have failed, even so, in my resolution, had it not chanced that my road to the
Depository of my machine lay past the eating-
house where I was wont to retire for bodily
refreshment from Flor and Fingelman's. As
I reached the door a hand touched my arm.
I looked round, startled, and saw the Grand
Vizier, outward bound from luncheon, with
his hairy hands, his goggle eyes, his shiny
black coat grown green on the seams, and his
false diamond pin shaped like a shoe of the
noble animal.

"Good-morning, miss," he said in a pert tone.

I echoed his salute, and made as though I
would pass on hurriedly. But I noted in

his accent, even from the three words he had spoken, a change of mien ; he was almost what for him might be deemed respectful.

" Look here," he went on, striding after me, and keeping abreast of me against my will. " That was a devilish clever letter of yours— to the governor, you know—a *devilish* clever letter ! "

" I am proud to have earned the approbation of so competent a critic," I answered in my chilliest voice. " Praise from Sir Hubert Stanley——"

He glanced at me with suspicion. I think his first and most flattered idea was that I mistook him for a distinguished baronet ; his second, neutral in tint, that I was mad ; his third, and most reluctant, that I was poking sly fun at him.

" Look here," he began again—it was his formula for introducing a fresh paragraph in his converse—" I've got an invitation for you. I've been looking about for you everywhere. Will you come with me on Thursday night, dress circle, at the Olympic ? "

He rolled it out impressively, as one who felt sure that the solemnity of the dress circle would subdue my stubborn neck.

"No, thanks," I answered; "I never go to theatres with casual acquaintances."

Then I walked on still faster, for I foresaw that I must often meet him in future, since our offices lay close together; and I judged it best to let him see at once I did not crave the honour of his society.

"Oh, but this is on the square," he went on. "You don't understand. You think I don't mean right by you because I am a gentleman in a position of Trust and Responsibility, and you are"—he was about to say "a type-writer girl," but he checked himself in time and substituted for it the phrase "a lady stenographer." "While you were at the office," he went on, "I couldn't treat you on equal terms, of course, because of my official position. But when I read that letter I saw at one glance you had brains; and I like a girl with brains, and I mean to walk out with one."

"Indeed?" I answered. "Then I advise you not to waste your valuable time on a woman who does not pant for that privilege."

He let his mouth drop open. "But it's a ticket for two," he expostulated, "given me by a friend of mine who takes a part in the piece. You'd better think twice. It isn't every day one gets a chance of a seat in the dress circle. And if I go at all I like to take a young lady."

This marked advance. I had gone up in the world. At Southa. ɔton Row I had been "a young person."

He continued to talk, and I continued to turn my coldest shoulder.

At last we reached the door of the Depository. The goggle eyes ogled me. I saw that some violent act was needful if I were to escape persecution at the man's hands in future. I paused by the step. "I am going in here," I said, bravely.

The Vizier did not observe the peculiar character of the shop as a shrine of St. Nicholas. "I will wait for you," he answered, waving one hairy hand with cheerful promptitude.

I braced myself up for a deadly thrust. "I have left my machine here," I went on in a cold clear voice, "and I am going in . . . to redeem it. I shall then carry it home. A Gentleman in a position of Trust and Responsibility will not like to be seen by my side as I carry it."

He glanced up at the mystic sign—one glance, no more. I saw his face grow pale.

To so respectable a man such conduct was inexplicable. Refuse a ticket for the dress circle, and yet——

I darted in, with the same fierce flush of shame and repugnance as before. But this time the need for getting rid of him had given me false courage.

When I emerged with the machine, a limp flaccid creature, half-dead with disgust, the Grand Vizier had melted away, disappeared among the phantoms. So again Apollo or St. Nicholas had saved me.

Our courses crossed afterwards in the street many times. But his tolerance of type-writer girls had its proper limits. He tacked across to the other side as I hove in sight lest he should be exposed to the risk of having to acknowledge a salute from so compromising a person.

I will say for St. Nicholas that though he has curious methods of bringing about the deliverance of those who trust him, he is a gentleman at heart, and he usually succeeds in the end in giving effect to his benevolent intentions.

CHAPTER XIII.

CONCERNING ROMEO.

It is a far cry from Verona to London. The ways of the Corso are not the ways of Pall Mall. Therefore, when I admit that my heart cried "A Romeo!" you are not to infer that I had fallen in love with him. I merely mean that I recognised in my new friend the type of man who might conceivably command my heart and me, should fate so will it.

When Romeo of Verona first saw his Juliet at the Capulets' masque, 'tis on record that, at first sight of her, he forgot fair Rosaline (for whose sake but one hour earlier he was dying to die), and seizing his new goddess's hand, assured her, without preamble or introduction, that his lips, two blushing pilgrims, ready stood to smooth that rough touch with a tender kiss; while Juliet, in return, was prepared to avow at a glance that if the stranger were married her grave was like to be her wedding bed. Those be the modes of Verona, as vouched by

K

Shakespeare. Our northern hearts, however, have not the instant electric responsiveness of Italian breasts. Love with us is the child, not the mother of acquaintance. And though I thought of my Romeo as Romeo from the first moment I beheld him, never calling him in my soul by any other name, yet 'twas but some prophetic fancy on my part. For many weeks he figured as no more than my employer.

Juliet of Verona, if I recollect aright, when she flung herself upon Romeo, was not yet full fourteen till Lammas night; at her age our northern maid, with her fair hair down, has conceived a romantic attachment for chocolate-creams and the prettiest of her governesses. I was twenty-two; and twenty-two, that mature age, takes time to consider. Moreover, it waits till its Romeo asks it.

For, pretend as we will, the plain truth is this: woman is plastic till the predestined man appears; then she takes the mould he chooses to impose upon her. Men make their own lives, women's are made for them. Why, one of my dearest friends at the Guild—an ethereal being—was wont to pace the garden with a vellum-covered Rossetti or Pater in her pocket, composing chants-royal to the moon and to divine love, till a man loomed on the horizon—a man in a Norfolk jacket, with a commission in the Guards and estates in the Midlands; whereupon she exchanged the Rossetti all at once for a blear-eyed ferret, and strolled about the lanes accompanied by a fox-terrier and a Cuban bloodhound. This is not poetical, but 'tis life as I have noted it.

To cut moralising short, I settled down at once to work at my Romeo's.

When I arrived there with my machine, more dead than alive with shame, the good-looking clerk carried it upstairs for me reverently. He was a comely youth, with a clean round face, Devonshire apple cheeks, and pleasant parsonage manners ; he came, indeed, as I discovered later, from an Exmoor rectory. A table was set for me in Romeo's own room. I feared to invade that sanctum. "Am I to sit right here ? " I asked. He smiled and answered, "Right there." So I took my place under protest. Thenceforth, I was part of the furniture of his study.

My life at Romeo's was a life of routine. Now routine (varied by outbreaks) is excellent for the nerves ; but it does not afford material for romance. It is the drab of life : art insists rather on the purple and scarlet.

K 2

So I make no apology for dealing with it here only in a few brief episodes.

All our history is episode, with blanks between, which just serve conveniently to divide the chapters.

At home, my social circle was limited to Mr. Commissioner Lin : my conversation to " Did 'ums, then ? did 'ums ? " At occasional intervals I dined with my aunt, who abode at Paddington : but I did not yearn to make that joy too common. My revered relation has all the vices of the decayed gentlewoman : unheroic vices, which interest nobody. She hoards bits of string, and half-sheets of note-paper. Her table, her ideas, and her discourse are meagre. She entertains angels, disguised as curates, and is a prop of the Deaconesses' Institute.

At the office, I had my seat in Romeo's own room. Poverty emancipates. It often occurred to me how different things would have been had my dear father lived, and had I remained a young lady. In that case, I could have seen Romeo at intervals only, under shelter of a chaperon ; as it was, no one hinted the faintest impropriety in the fact that the type-writer girl was left alone with him half the day in the privacy of his

study. Not that this freedom gave me much
occasion (at first) for talk with Romeo. He
was courtesy itself, and by nature conversible :
but his chivalrous feelings, and his sense
of my isolation, made him chary of speaking.
He dictated all day, or left me to transcribe ;
but he seldom broke silence save on matters
of business.

Nevertheless, from the outset, he was
markedly kind to me. I had two nice boys
at hand to run errands and carry my notes ;
one, a skimpy London imp, compact of saucy
humour ; I called him Puck : the other,
a slender lad of fifteen, pale, delicate, girlishly
pretty, with long straw-coloured hair and
a distracted manner, whom I rechristened
Ariel. Romeo gradually adopted this trick
of speech from me. It is a habit of mine (as
you may have observed) to invent names
for my friends; and these generally stick—
I suppose because I borrow them as a rule
from the poets, who have classified us into
types which recur perennially.

After I had been at the office a few weeks,
I happened one day to slip into some Ameri-
canism. Though I have seen little of America
(having gone there but once on a visit to my
father's folk at Salem when I was not quite

fifteen) I have inherited from my ancestry not a few Massachusetts idioms, one or other of which I sometimes let drop, unconsciously to myself, in the course of conversation. Romeo snapped at the word at once. " Why, you must be a New Englander ! "

" Not quite," I answered, flushing. " My father was born at Salem, an American citizen ; but he became naturalised in England young, and was a British officer."

" Not in the army ? " Romeo cried, surprised.

"Yes," I answered. "Why not? A colonel."

I grew hot as I spoke. For the first and only time, I think Romeo doubted me. "Then you—must have—a pension," he broke out, slowly.

It was partly desire to avoid telling the truth, partly a certain native love of mystification—or rather of piquing other people's curiosity; but I answered with a touch of defiance, " An officer's daughter loses her pension on marriage. I may be married, perhaps—or separated—or a widow." And I bent down over my work to hide my heightened colour.

He gazed at me for a second ; his eye fell on my left hand ; then he glanced away.

I could see him saying to himself he had no right to cross-question me. But interest in me prevailed. He drew near, and stood over me. "You must forgive my persistence," he said, gently, in his modulated voice—each syllable clear as crystal—"but I feel constrained to ask you. Have you really a pension? . . . . For if so, you have misled me."

I looked up at him with proud eyes. My father's blood rose hot in me. "I must tell you the truth," I said, "or you will think I am ashamed of my father. I am not ashamed; I am proud of him. He was an English colonel; but I have no pension. He was a very brave man. He threw up his commission, in time of war, at a moment of danger, almost in face of the enemy, because he would not carry out orders which seemed to him unjust. And he died of anxiety and fever just after, on the West Coast of Africa."

"I remember the case. Pray forgive me. It was cruel of me to drive you."

"Not at all. I am glad you did. Now you will understand better."

I rose, flushed, and faced him. "They say a soldier should resign his conscience into the keeping of the Queen's advisers. My father

could not. He felt wrong was being done.
He would not make his judgment blind. He
left me poor by it; and I am proud of it—
proud of him."

"You have reason to be proud," Romeo
answered. "I recall it all now. His previous
record showed it was courage, not cowardice.
I honoured him for it at the time—though
the world thought otherwise."

"Thank you," I said in a low voice. "May
I go now? It is nearly five. And I feel,
after this, I can do no more work this evening."

He opened the door for me and bowed even
more respectfully than usual. There was
sympathy in every movement. I felt he
understood. I felt I had made a friend. I
felt, still more surely than before, that *this*
was my Romeo.

CHAPTER XIV.

"NOW BARABBAS WAS A PUBLISHER.

I REGRET to say that from that day forth
Romeo was more marked in his courtesy to
me than ever. His manner had always a
tinge of sweet antique courtliness ; but now
he surpassed himself. I regret it, I say,
because I was afraid I recognised in this
courtesy some lingering undercurrent of class
feeling. The dear fellow would have been
polite to a type-writer girl from the dregs of
the people, no doubt—he did not know how
to be less than polite to anyone ; but he was
politer still when he understood that I was an
officer's daughter, and (as he learned a week
later) that my mother had sprung from a great
Anglo-Indian family. This was treason to his
principles ; for Romeo, as he had said, was
more than half a socialist ; but I condoned that
fault for the sake of his unvarying kindness.

Besides, I think he thought well of me
because I was loyal to my father's memory.

As though anyone who had known my dear father could have been otherwise !

Romeo published for Sidney Trevelyan. From the moment when I first noticed "An Heir of the Plantagenets" among the rows of books in glazed paper covers in the pigeon-holes, I had always longed to be present some day when the famous novelist came in to discuss royalties or *éditions de luxe* with his publisher. Sidney Trevelyan's name was like Charing Cross or Hyde Park Corner—a familiar piece of public property. One afternoon I had my will. I was seated at my table, clicking away at some letters, when I heard on the stairs a rich strident voice, diffusing itself very loud in clear shrill accents. I know not which struck me most, its richness or its stridency. It was a sonorous voice, which one turn of a note would have made unendurable. "He is in his lair?" it said, filling the room. " Plotting schemes to suck my blood ? Then I will track him to his earth—the young vampire. My dear Barabbas, how are you ? "

He burst into the sanctum, a whirlwind of a man—large, loose-limbed, masterful, with a restless grey eye, and a huge mop of brown hair, shot with threads of russet. Romeo rose to greet him. He flung himself into a chair. It creaked beneath his elephantine weight. I left off clicking at once, and went on with a piece of long-hand transcription. Or rather, to be frank, I feigned to transcribe, though my pen was inkless.

As a rule, when authors came, 'twas my place to leave the study for awhile, and take refuge with Puck and Ariel in the anteroom. But as the great man entered—two yards of humanity, double width—Romeo signed to me to remain, with a quick movement of the eyebrow. He knew my wish, and was kind enough to remember it. I counted it to him for righteousness.

Sidney Trevelyan sniffed, and scanned the room, with its Oriental hangings, and its scent of cedar-wood. "A nice den, Barabbas, a nice den!" he observed, in a condescending tone; "an Ali Baba's cave, rich with bones of authors; vastly improved since the days of the old robber!"

Romeo winced. Like myself, he respected his father.

"You have garnished it afresh," the great novelist continued, "from the spoils of the Egyptians. You have decked yourself in purple and fine linen! Well, 'tis well you

should be comfortable in this world, no doubt:
for in the next——But I refrain from painting
a Tartarean picture. Dante has done it so
well before me that, like the grocer in my
street, he defies competition. I see you, my
dear Barabbas," he raised his voice still
louder, almost lapsing into a falsetto, "I see
you lolling here in Eastern opulence, bathed in
Cyprian perfumes, and fanned by obsequious
Circassian odalisques "—I *felt* him glance my
way, though my eyes were fixed on my paper ;
" I see you, like the sultan in Shelley's *Hellas*,
surrounded by large-eyed houris, of volup-
tuous bosoms, who strew your restless pillow
with opiate flowers—I call your pillow restless, my dear fellow, partly because that was
Shelley's epithet, if memory serves me, but
partly also because a publisher (especially a
young one) can scarcely expect to enjoy
sound slumber ; later on, no doubt, as he
becomes hardened in crime, he sleeps as well
as a digestion impaired by old port permits ;
but at first, remorse must disturb his fitful
rest—I see you, I say, with opiate flowers on
your couch stripped—what was the rhyme ?
—ah, yes, 'flowers,' 'pillow'—stripped from
orient bowers by the Indian billow. That is
the picture — *here*. But at last comes the

awakening." He struck a dramatic attitude,
and held up one hand ; he had impressive
fat hands, which seemed always in evidence.
"You start from your sleep like Mahmood.
'Man the seraglio—guard! Make fast the
gate!' You dream yourself still lapped in
Eastern magnificence. Then . . . . ha!
what's this? An odour of brimstone—a
pallid whiff of blue flame—Mephistopheles
smiling grimly on the victim he has landed—
you know where you are—unlike the current
hero of music-hall romance—you stretch dim
hands of fear and grope—you sink down,
down, down, on a couch of liquid fire. 'All
is lost! Why was I ever a publisher?' In
which of his circles did Dante place publishers?
Was it not close between the avaricious and
the prevaricators? But aloft in the empyrean,
pillowed on purple cloud, meanwhile, I enjoy
that delight upon which Tertullian insisted
as a prime element in the ecstasy of the Blest
—the delight of beholding you——But your
satellites overhear me! Sense of discipline
forbids! Barabbas," he waved his hand, " I
draw a veil over your future condition !"

He paused for want of breath. Most fat
men are sluggish : this mountain of flesh was
alive and volcanic in every atom. Romeo

began in his soft voice, "And on what particular conspiracy of crime have you come to-
day to consult the habitual criminal ? "

Sidney Trevelyan smiled. He liked to be
taken in his mood. " Well, my business,"
he said, "is, as you anticipate, a fresh raid
against the purses of the Philistines. We
must spoil them, my dear Barabbas ; we must
spoil them, in unison. Here, our interests
are identical. They have taken two thousand,
I see, of the three-volume 'Mahatmas.' That's
not enough ; you must issue at once a six-
shilling edition. Grovelling beasts, prone in
the mud they love, what do they mean by
rejecting this so great salvation? Let Mudies
see to it ! I shall answer their neglect by
flinging back ' Mahatmas' in their teeth for six
shillings. I know whence it comes, this re-
buff : those ignorant parrots, the critics. They
toss at me ever their parrot cry of ' Artificial,
artificial ! ' Their own thoughts grub and
grunt in the mud of their sty, and they blame
it to the eagle that he should circle about
gleaming icy peaks in clear ether. ' Un-
natural,' they say ; ' Overloaded.' That man
Snigg, or Snagg, or Snogg—something Teutonic and unlovely—I decline to remember
his honoured name—he reviewed me in the

Parthenon. He has no wings himself, and therefore he thinks flight an indecent gambolling. But what do I care for the whole crew ? Not an obolus, not a doit—neither for Snagg nor Bagg, neither for Archer nor Parcher."

He paused again to catch breath. In the lull, Romeo put in quietly, " It is too soon, in my opinion, for a cheap edition."

" No, Barabbas, it is not ; it is the pyschological moment. The world awaits it with hushed breath. Six shillings—bound in cloth —Irish linen—dark green—a subtle shade— a shade I have in my mind's eye—like lavender leaves in spring, when the sap mounts emerald through sea-hoary stems. You catch my idea? A green not wholly green, not altogether blue, not grey, not glaucous, but something of all, and more than all ; with a cunning design by that mad young Belgian —withy-bands that twist into interlacing dragons ; the title in their midst, in somewhat Celtic letters."

He broke off abruptly. Once more I could feel him glance my way. I seemed to see through the back of my head. I was sensitive to his movements.

Suddenly, he burst out in a quite different voice, snorting like a war-horse : " Send that young woman away!" he cried, executing a sort of ponderous rhinoceros-dance before me. "Send her away! I tell you I can't stand her. I won't have her scribbling there and making notes of all I say. She's a para-graphist—a paragraphist : the vilest spawn on God's earth, a paragraphist! What do you mean by setting spavined shorthand writers to report my *obiter dicta ?*" He advanced towards me, striding : I had risen hurriedly. "Go off!" he cried, waving his hands at me as if I were a gadfly. "Go off! I won't be listened to and paragraphed. I could feel you paragraphing me. Away, young woman : away with you." And by dint of sheer bulk, he drove me before him.

Romeo opened the door for me. He spoke with deference. "I think, Miss Appleton," he said, " you had better take a seat in the ante-room for the moment, as your presence here seems to disturb Mr. Trevelyan."

I went out, mystified. As the door closed behind me, I heard the great man snort again. "Now, really, Barabbas, if you choose to keep dusky Samian slaves chained in your lair for your hours of leisure, you should have the decency to unchain them when fellow-conspirators come in with proposals for a joint campaign against Askelon."

I sat in the anteroom for half an hour. Ariel gazed in my face with sympathetic inquiry. " The old bear was rude ? " he asked at last, in a low voice.

"I might almost call him so."

"It is his way," Ariel replied. "He seems to wipe his shoes on one."

" But he's not a bad old chap, either," Puck put in. " He chucked me half-a-crown once for going a message for him."

"And called you a Tartar-nosed imp," Ariel added ; "and hit you in the eye with it."

" He is a very great genius," I observed, sententiously, half to salve my own offended dignity.

" But a genius is a man," Ariel remarked. And I felt he had reason.

Twenty minutes later, the famous writer emerged. He cast a scowl at me in passing. "Change your type-writer woman ! " he said curtly to Romeo. " Good-bye, my dear Barabbas. Rob on, rob ever." His broad back vanished down the staircase like a sinking hippopotamus.

"Well ? " Romeo asked, with an anxious face, as I returned to my post when the tornado had passed. "Now you have seen him, what do you think of Sidney Trevelyan ?"

"I think," I said, "I would rather be a Barabbas than a Byron."

CHAPTER XV.

FRESH LIGHT ON ROMEO.

"SIDNEY TREVELYAN is a great man," Romeo said to me later ; "but his ideas are *too* great —especially his idea of his own greatness. This taints life for him : he moves in an atmosphere of social suspicion. 'Tis his fixed belief that all the world is always thinking of him, when it is really doing as he does— thinking of itself. He imagines reporters as a sultan imagines poison, or as a tsar imagines nihilists ; he scents a paragraphist in every hedge, and a critic in every stranger." Which explains, I suppose, his odd behaviour.

But my own opinion is that he needed an audience ; I could catch it in his voice that he meant me to overhear ; because I affected to be absorbed in my work he thought I was not listening, and that made him angry.

Romeo was kindness itself to me ; yet I dare say I might never have grown to know him better had it not been for the special providence of an accident—or the accident of a special providence; put it whichever way best suits your philosophy.

Straying one afternoon through the Cretan labyrinth of Soho, I happened to note a young girl, very poorly dressed, but with the air of a lady, staring in at a confectioner's. Her face struck a chord. I ransacked my memory for it in vain. Then I recalled in a flash where I had met her before; she was the girl whom I had passed on the stairs at Romeo's on the day when I went to apply for the situation; the girl whom I had supplanted in the struggle for existence.

Her shrinking figure, her whipped air, made me turn to ask an inevitable question: "Have you found work yet?"

"No, none," she said dejectedly. "How came you to know I wanted it?"

I explained where I had seen her, and how I had heard or guessed her errand. She seemed unduly grateful. My heart was touched, for though I doubt not you think me, on my own evidence, a heartless young woman, I *have* a heart, after all, when aught occurs to rouse it. I reflected at once how even my gentle Romeo had said of this poor child that she was hope-

lessly incompetent. Still, the incompetent
have mouths to feed, and bodies to clothe,
and possibly, also, souls to save, like the
rest of us. The struggle for life has not
quite choked out my soul (if I have one).
I invited her to my room for a cup of tea, and
an ounce of sympathy. Her gratitude was a
satire on Christian charity in this town of
London. I found she could type fairly well,
though quite unintelligently, like a well-
trained Chinaman; but she had no machine
of her own, and no money to buy one; nor
could she undertake work where dictation
was necessary; though, given a copy, she
could reproduce each word with mechanical
fidelity.

It flashed across me at once that all day
long I was away at Romeo's, and did not
need my machine. "Better come here," I
said, "and use it. I will find you manu-
scripts to transcribe; we have plenty of such
work to give away at the office."

She fawned on me like a dog accustomed
to ill-treatment, and for once used kindly.
The ravenous way in which she ate bread
and butter would have satisfied even the
Charity Organisation Society as to the
genuineness of her hunger. She was pain-

fully grateful. Her gratitude distressed me.
After that we became fast friends. It is
true, she was terrified at the first smell of
tobac—— But I forget; that delinquency
I have hitherto concealed from you. However, she used my machine every day, and
I helped her in the evenings. Pale, blue-
eyed, colourless, with thin hair tied up in a
knot the size of a nutmeg, she was built on
the same lines as Michaela (whom I always
remembered), but with this trifling difference
—that Michaela was rich, while my new little
friend had not a cent to bless herself with.
One was bound in Morocco, with gilt edges ;
the other, a cheap edition, in paper covers.

Her name was Elsie, her front name,
that is to say ; for she had another, I suppose, a surname ; but I took no heed of it.
Surnames lie on the surface of things, and do
not interest me. They are of this age, utilitarian ; while I, who dwell ever in Once-
upon-a-time, care little save for the persons
and dates of fairyland. We give each other
surnames, indeed, only so long as we are
mutual phantoms ; once pierce to the under-
lying realities of human life, and we call
one another by pet names, like so many
children.

In time Elsie became to me a sort of
adopted daughter. She was older than I to
be sure ; but her helplessness and incompetence inspired in me at last that sense of
motherliness which we women love—does it
not come out in us even toward our dolls in
childhood ? Her affection was canine. I
found work for her from a type-writing office
hard by—simple work, selected with a special
eye to her limitations. She toiled at it with
that patience which one observes in the
squirrel who turns the unceasing treadmill of
his cage ; for minds of a certain calibre prefer
routine, which would kill a thinking animal,
to any task that calls for the slightest exercise
of intelligence. As long as she was permitted
to go on copying like a machine, Elsie was
perfectly happy : a doubt or a query seemed
(as she said) to comb her brain ; she lost
heart before an alternative.

I spent little time in my room myself, save
for the strict necessaries of sleep and breakfast ; at other times I was driven out of it by
a work of art on the walls—the Portrait of
a Locket. It represented, or rather repre-
sents (for doubtless it still exists), a gold
locket and chain, reposing on an ample
black silk bosom, with a woman's face and

hands in the background. The face and hands, so far as can be seen, are fat and placid ; the hands crossed ; the face feature- less. Flesh-tints and modelling, however, cast much rude work upon the imagination. I had not courage enough to suggest the removal of this gem to my landlady, who valued it highly as "a real oil-painting"; but it, and two vases, drove me out, I will not say to the public-house, but to the public buildings. I retired at odd moments to my drawing-room in the National Gallery, or to the hospitable electric light of the British Museum. Elsie, on the other hand, was not repelled by the locket or the lady. I had now no use for my machine, and she worked on it constantly. She and the Commissioner struck up a violent friendship. It did her good to have some living creature at hand in the room to whom she could talk in the inter- vals of click-clicking. To enlarge her circle I added in time a starling and a canary, whom we christened Beef and Mustard. The canary was Mustard because of his colour, and the starling Beef because there was so much more of him.

One of the points which had barred Elsie's way in the matter of obtaining employment,

she felt profoundly convinced, was her religious opinions, which were soundly narrow.
This happily enabled her, like Rothenburg,
to gild her penury with the halo of the
martyr.

For myself, I suspect that incompetence
had more to do with her failure than religious
prejudice; but that is a private conviction.
She was a Positivist, or a Plymouth Sister, or a
member of some other uncanny small sect; I
will plead guilty to discriminating ill these
minor brands of creed ; I am hazy as to the
true distinction between General and Particular
Baptists (though, perhaps, a Particular Baptist
uses soap) ; and I always mix up Sweden-
borgians with Irvingites.   It was a surprise
to Elsie to find that her form of faith seemed
to me a question of small import either way.
I hold that most men are human, and, still
more, most women.   My tolerance astonished
her.   When I suggested that perhaps at that
very minute Swedenborg and Irving, John
Knox and Thomas à Kempis, might perchance
be gazing down upon us with kindly eyes
and an amused smile from some sequestered
garden bench in one of the spacious pleasure-
grounds of the Celestial City, where they
sat in rapt converse with the soul of John

Glas, who first prospected her own strictly provincial path to Paradise, she turned her face to me with mingled delight and terror. My view seemed to her sweet but highly heterodox. She refused to her God a breadth of sympathy which she instinctively admired in a fellow-creature.

One evening I came home and found Elsie at work on a piece of transcription which was evidently too deep for her. It was poetry, she said, in an awed whisper: she had been given it at the office under a promise of secrecy. But the arrangement of the long and short lines of complicated stanzas, which needed some care in the adjustment of margins, was evidently beyond her. She looked tired and worried, and was mildly tearful. "Besides, dear," she said, smoothing my hair, "there are such difficult words in it—words nobody could spell; not even you, I believe—such as *myrrh* with two *r*'s and an *h*. I can't manage them anyhow."

"Dictate to me," I said; "I can write for a bit. I've not done much to-day, and I'm hardly the least bit tired."

She dictated several strophes. I was not surprised that she found the words hard. "Chrysoprase" "mandragora," "anaglyph,"

" Libitina "—these lay some miles outside poor little Elsie's vocabulary.

At first I noticed only the rare richness of the language, the many-faceted words, set like jewels so as to show their full beauty; gradually, as she dictated, I began to be aware that the verses she read aloud to me in her infantile sing-song were not merely rhyme but also poetry. I do not pretend to the name of critic; but I judged them to be written with limpid felicity. They had that artlessness which comes of the apt use of the perfect word without show of effort. Each noun and adjective fell so naturally into its place that one fancied the writer could have used no other—till one began to reflect that only studious care results in so absolute a sense of inevitability. And the poems were statuesque; they had none of the tropical exuberance of our time; they were Greek in their austerity.

" Who is the author ? " I asked, curious to know the name of the poet with this Ionic note, new to our English Helicon.

" They didn't tell me. They wished me not to know. He particularly desired that his verses should be kept secret."

She went on dictating in her mechanical

way.   My hand struck the keys rapidly.   At
last she paused, near the close of a curious
variant on the Spenserian stanza.   " There's
a word I can't make out," she murmured.
" ' True woman has the magic ' *something——*"

I took the manuscript from her hands.

" True woman has the magic Midas gift ;
Touched by her hand, dull clay transmutes to molten gold."

But that was not what made me give a
sudden cry of surprise, and then turn red as
a peony.   The verses were written in Romeo's
hand.   And Romeo was their author.

In a second I was buried in them, like a
bee in a crocus.   I felt he was even more to
me than before.   I had believed him a publisher; now I knew him a poet.   No Barabbas, but a Byron.

How long I lay awake in my garret that
night—thinking of whom but of Romeo !

CHAPTER XVI.

I TRY LITERATURE.

NEXT morning at lunch time, as I crossed Long Acre, I caught a glimpse of Michaela, in the gondola of London, steering rapidly northward. A big summer hat, all wild roses and gossamer, half hid her face, like a wild rose itself, pink and white and delicate.

At sight of me she recognised me, and stopped her hansom short for a second to grasp my hand. I was pleased at her remembrance. She had come from Waterloo, she said, and was hurrying now to catch a train at Euston. She looked radiantly happy; I told her so. Her face flushed with pleasure; she leaned forward and confided to me in a thrilling whisper that she was to be married in the autumn to the friend whom she had lost on the day I first met her. I wished her joy, and waved my hand. She vanished, smiling, towards Euston and the Unknown, a phantom once more among the flickering phantoms.

Happy at her happiness, I tripped back to Romeo's. She was an airy little thing of gauze and bergamot, like a breath of fairy-land.

That afternoon Romeo's talk to me was more human than usual. It was always plain that he wan'ed to talk, but a sense of the official nature of our relation restrained him often. To-day he spoke much of woman's place in literature. So many women, he said, wrote of life with a note of personality rare among men. They put more heart in it. Even squalor or crime grew less base when they handled it.

Half unconsciously to myself, I murmured under my breath,

"True woman has the magic Midas gift ;
Touched by her hand, dull clay transmutes to molten gold."

I murmured it quite low ; but he caught at the words with a sharp gasp. "Where did you see that ?" he asked quickly.

I was forced to confess, "The lines oc-curred in some verses a little friend of mine —I told you of her some days since—had for copy yesterday from a type-writing office."

I tried not to let him know more ; but, for a woman, I am a poor dissembler ; my colour or the trembling of my lips betrayed me.

"Did you see the manuscript?" he inquired.

"Yes; I helped her to transcribe it."

"They promised secrecy!" he cried.

"And you shall have it," I answered.

He paused a moment. "But *you* were the last person I would have wished to see them," he went on, his face twitching.

I knew why. In some of them an allusion, a description—here, a blue-veined eyelid; there, a gloss like a swallow's wing on a woman's smooth hair—had seemed to me familiar.

He paced up and down the tawny carpet for awhile. Then he broke out once more. "I have written verse since I was a boy," he said. "It has ever been my ambition to be found worthy of the crown of poet. But if I printed these lyrics under my own name, what use? I could but give a handle for Sidney Trevelyan to ask in the *Saturday Review* 'Is Barabbas also among the prophets?' Nobody will take a publisher's rhymes seriously. So I decided to issue mine under an assumed name, and with another firm, that critics might at least be rude to them on their merits. For that purpose I had them type-written— and not by you. I am sorry you have seen them."

"And I am glad," I answered. "You may not care for my opinion ; but these verses are masterpieces of handicraft. You have the rare gift of reticence. Besides, you understand the fitness of words ; you appreciate their melting shades of tone ; you feel the emotional atmosphere with which each is girdled."

"Thank you," he said, checking himself. "And *you* are one of the few whose praise I value. You speak well of my work for the qualities I strive to have, not for those I know I have not."

From that day forth he was much more at home with me. You see, we shared a Secret in common.

When his volume came out, several months later, it made no stir in the world ; but it gained the approbation of five or six out of the twenty-three men and women in England who love poetry. It will yet be known, I think ; for though the public often flock together like sheep after some noisy impostor, true poetry is always forced upon them from above by the chosen few who can discover and impose it. The few are frequently obscure, and bear no hall-mark ; but they know one another by the two gifts which make a critic—insight and foresight.

My knowledge of this book drew me nearer to Romeo. Having once accepted the fact that I knew of his work, he consulted me time and again as to type and paper—sometimes also as to the choice of an epithet or a point of cadence, when two equally-balanced alternatives divided his preference. Should it be *lurid* or *livid*? was *ruddy* or *russet* the better? This led us into talks not altogether official. Though always reticent, he began to treat me less as a type-writer and more as a woman.

This quality of reticence, which I observed in Romeo's self no less than in his work, impressed me profoundly. I admired his quiet strength, his calm, his urbanity. I am not urbane myself, and I fear I must grant that I am rather vehement than strong; therefore I respected all the more these traits in Romeo. One honours one's complement above one's counterpart. He never spoke strongly; he reserved strength for action. A week or two after Sidney Trevelyan's visit I asked him one day whether the cheap edition of "Mahatmas" was going forward. He smiled his restrained smile, and answered, "No, certainly not; I never intended it."

"But Mr. Trevelyan was so urgent, so instant; he had quite made up his mind."

M

" Yes ; that is unimportant. The moment had not arrived, and I told him so, calmly. He is a rock when opposed ; but calmness, like faith, can move mountains. I did not oppose him at the time ; opposition just then could only have irritated him. I saw the state of his soul ; he came to me, seething internally with suppressed wrath at the critics. I let him blow off steam ; in such circumstances I judge it unwise to sit upon the safety-valve. He opened his heart and had it out, flinging many hard jibes at me and at the public. That relieved the tension. I let three days pass ; then I wrote an ultimatum, stating quietly what I thought. He gave in at once. The cheap edition shall not appear till the autumn."

Such masculine absence of fussiness pleased me.

Once or twice when I discussed with him he asked me seriously why I had never written. I laughed off his assault. He returned to the charge ; so much racy material going to waste in my own adventures. I told him of my work among the East-End slop-makers ! " Ready-made stories," was his verdict. I doubted my own faculty. He was sure I possessed it.

This encouraged me to narrate my experience at Pinfold. "Anarchists !—and
they blamed me because I could not fall in
love to order ! "

"You are an intrepid young lady," Romeo
said. "Do you know, I doubt if you quite
realise always in what galleys you have
embarked."

"I think I do," I answered : "but I have
confidence in myself and my guardian angel."

He urged me to try my hand at a short
story of the modern girl who earns her own
living in London—"for example, this little
friend who uses your type-writer," he added
with a clever side-thrust ; I was grateful to
him for thus diverting the theme from my
own personality : "there is no more pathetic
figure in our world to-day than the common
figure of the poor young lady, crushed between classes above and below, and left with
scarce a chance of earning her bread with
decency."

"I fear," I said, "I have no knack of
pathos ; even at difficult turns I am apt to
see rather the humorous than the tragic side
of things."

"So I note. But why not try ; your own
late adventures, for instance ? "

M 2

I felt that that romance had not yet reached its *dénoûment;* but I refrained from telling him so. I promised to make an attempt, however, with one of my earlier East-End reminiscences, or else with a little vignette of the infant anarchists, unsullied by soap, pulling Commissioner Lin's tail, while their sisters turned the House that Jack built into Czech and Yiddish.

For a week or two I worked hard in my stray moments at this my poor little literary first-born. I put its phrases in curl-papers till I was sick of twisting them. When it was ripe for the birth, I confess I thought meanly of it. Mine own, but a poor thing, to reverse Touchstone's saying : I brought it to Romeo, trembling. He read it and was enthusiastic. For the first time now I felt sure he really cared for me ; what else could so have blinded his critical faculty ? For he was a judicious reader.

He praised it as if it were the work of a consummate artist. His encouragement was unstinted. I will not repeat what he said as to my style ; you, who are reading my second effort in that line, would be painfully aware how much personal partiality must have warped his judgment.

"It is so breezy," he said. "You write open-air English."

"I learnt it on the moors, among the whins," I answered.

"This eclogue must go into the magazine!" he cried; for, like most other great houses, the firm published one of its own.

I drew a line at that. "Oh, no," I cried, flushing. "You are too kind, too generous. I will not allow it to be printed where— where personal acquaintance and your recommendation may disturb the editor's calmer opinion. I must send it to someone else. Then it will be weighed for what it is worth, and if it is accepted, I shall know on what grounds."

"But I shall be sorry to lose it," he exclaimed; "for the magazine's own sake. When one discovers a new writer, one wishes to keep the full credit of the discovery."

I looked down to hide my burning cheeks. "No, no," I said firmly. "You are too flattering—too good. Your"——I paused to think how I could best word it; "your knowledge of me predisposes you too much in my favour."

He looked at me and hesitated. "Not my

knowledge alone," he corrected; "my . . . friendship, my——"

He did not say "affection"; but we raised our eyes in unison; and in a flash of those eyes each knew that he meant it.

There was a long pause. I was aware of my heart, which called attention to its existence by a violent throbbing. I went back to my machine and began typing mechanically. Then he added all at once, "But quite apart from that, I *want* this story; I want the honour of publishing it, because I see it is a good one."

I went on clicking. "You cannot separate these things," I said, without looking up. "A person is a totality. We do not know, ourselves, how much of any feeling is due to this cause, and how much to that. Nothing ever goes wholly free from either fear or favour. But I have made up my mind. I shall send it to *The Pimlico.*"

I sent it in the end; and, to my great joy, not unmixed with surprise, the editor accepted it, in a chastening letter. He did not say, like Romeo, "a gem of English"; he called it on the contrary, "high-spirited if flippant"; but he printed it none the less, and forwarded me a cheque for twelve guineas.

Twelve guineas ! Such wealth seemed to me almost incredible. I felt like an Argonaut.

Still, Romeo was vexed. "We ought to have had it," he said ; "for, after all, you were *my* discovery."

CHAPTER XVII.

A DRAWN BATTLE.

It was about this time, if I recollect aright (for *I* am the girl who does not keep a diary), that Romeo invited me to dinner.

I have two reasons for my avoidance of the besetting sin of diary-writing. The first is that I am usually dog-tired with work when evening comes, so that to ask me to fill in a journal with the day's events is like asking a galley-slave to take a scull in a pleasure-boat after his toil is over. The second is that if you keep no diary it cannot be used in evidence against you. As yet, 'tis true, by rigid self-examination, I have steered clear of capital crimes ; but I remember always Ophelia's wise saw, "We know what we are ; we know not what we may be."

Romeo invited me with caution, and tentatively. He began by remarking, as if for no special reason, that he was giving a dinner next week at the Savoy—a dinner devised for

a particular purpose. Then he added after a
while that his mother would be there. This to
inspire confidence, dear fellow! as though I
ever doubted him. Next he inquired in a rather
timid voice whether, if his mother picked me
up by the way in her brougham, I would mind
joining the party. "My mother has not called
upon you yet," he murmured in an apologetic
parenthesis, looking up at me askance from
under his ridged eyebrows with an interro-
gative lid; "but—perhaps you would waive
that." From the way he said it I could read
much. I felt instinctively she was a black-satin
old lady of the straightest sect; Romeo had
implored her to call; she had refused point-
blank to go and see a type-writer girl who
lived in one room in an impossible street in
Soho. Romeo had begged and prayed; the
mother had presented the true stiff neck of the
black-satin order. Then Romeo had planned
this dinner as a means of introducing me, confident (dear boy) that if once we were brought
together, his mother—well, would think as
much of me as he did. Poor purblind
Romeo! I pitied him for that. How little
had he fathomed black-satin psychology!

I hesitated a moment. Not on Romeo's
account, nor even on the mother's—I do not

fear the smoothest black satin; but because of
the mere material difficulty of a gown, which
just at first rose insuperable. Otherwise I
thought so much of Romeo now—he had
begun to play so large a part in the unwritten
dramas of my future with which I lulled myself to sleep—that I felt at all costs I must be
present at this dinner and face the mother.
A mother is almost inevitable; the sooner one
gets over her, like measles, the better.

I had one evening dress, or the ghost of
one, which had descended to me from the
days when I was a lady. Its sleeves carried
date; but the bodice and skirt were of that
fanciful kind which is above the fashion, and
therefore never either in it or out of it. The
colour was sweet—white, shot with faint
streaks of the daintiest pink, like the first
downy stage of budding willow catkins. On
the other hand, I was still in mourning for
my dear father. Had I loved him less I
should have shrunk from wearing that gown;
but my sorrow was not of the sort that
measures itself by yards of crape, which is
why I have troubled you with it so little in
this narrative. I reflected a moment; then I
answered, "Yes; it will give me great pleasure."

That it gave Romeo great pleasure was visibly written on his face. He had expected a *no*, and was delighted at my acceptance. I knew by his eyes he had anticipated and even exaggerated the dress difficulty. I did not misinterpret his pleased look, however. I never thought Romeo was in love with me ; I knew he was interested in me, both personally and as a possible authoress ; and I saw he wished much to bring me officially into his mother's circle. More than that, I did not believe, or rather, if I am to tell you the precise truth, I thought Romeo was falling in love with me by slow steps, but mistaking his love for mere interest and friendliness.

For a week I was a woman, not merely a type-writer. I worked hard at that gown, first planning, then executing my alterations. Dear little Elsie helped me with it like a Trojan. Nay, in cutting out and fitting she displayed or developed unexpected talent. When dress was in question she was no longer stupid ; the woman in her grew ; she showed taste and skill ; indeed, I have noted in life, throughout, that taste has no necessary connection, direct or inverse, with intelligence or stupidity ; it is a native endowment which

may break out anywhere. She was glad it was
a dinner, not a dance ; her religious opinions
would not have sanctioned her assisting me
with a ball-dress. But all sects alike ap-
prove the habit of feeding. I must admit that
when it came to the details of my gown she
showed herself at once most frankly worldly.
Elsie had little chance of making dresses for
herself, poor child; but she aided me with her
needle and her advice till I was truly grateful.
The way she reorganised the sleeves to a
Parisian model made one believe in alchemy.
We spent a few shillings on new tulle and
lining. Every evening we had an orgy of
dressmaking : whole packets of pins, snippets
of silk on the floor. Before the end of the
week we had transformed that old gown of
mine into a joy for ever. It was better than
new ; as it fell in soft folds the blush showed
on the ridge and cream-white in the hollows.
When I tried it on, Elsie bent over me enrap-
tured. "You dear thing!" she cried, hugging
me (to the danger of the tulle), " I always
knew you were pretty, but I never knew till
now you were splendidly beautiful."

And I will honestly admit that the frock
became me.

The day arrived at last. Elsie came round

to help me dress my hair. We made more of
this dinner than I should have made of being
presented in the days of my grandeur—such
as it was. Dear little Elsie had brought me
some flowers from a friend's garden at Ealing,
choice sweet-scented flowers, with a background of maidenhair. If I had believed her,
I would have thought no fairy princess ever
looked more radiant than I looked that evening; and, indeed, our joint efforts on the gown
repaid us with interest. When the last touch
had been given Elsie kissed me on both
cheeks. "He will propose to-night," she
whispered. "I know he will: he can't help
himself, dear. You *are* so captivating!" I
blushed, for I had never mentioned his name
to Elsie; but then, I forgot that Elsie too was
a woman.

At ten minutes to eight the brougham
arrived at the door. Never before had our
street beheld so distinguished an equipage.
This was unfortunate, for the children next
door came to gaze at me with dirty faces and
unaffected interest, exclaiming, "Oh, my, don't
she look a reel lidy?" as I made a rush for the
carriage.

Romeo's mother was precisely what I
had painted her—a Lady Montague of the

severest, with coffee-coloured point-lace, a
Cornelia one shade too stout for the mother
of the Gracchi. Her smooth white hair
looked not gentle, but forbidding; she listened
to what I said with well-bred reserve: too stiff
to acquiesce, too polite to contradict, too stony
to show interest.

At the hotel, we were ushered into a handsome private room, most gracefully decorated
with crimson arabesques on white panelling.
The party consisted of Romeo and his mother
with some six or eight more (including a prebendary), among whom the chief guests
seemed to be a certain amiable-faced Lady
Donisthorpe and her husband, Sir Everard.
I name them in this order, for though the
husband was a man of some force and character
—early English, comfortable—Lady Donisthorpe, like Paul, was the chief speaker. She
seemed what is called "a womanly woman"
—one of those tranquil women with soft,
rounded outlines, who look like wax, but
within are flint. She reminded me most of
all of a pouter pigeon.

She apologised much because dear Meta
could not come. It was *such* a disappointment. The poor child had been taken ill—
nothing serious she was glad to say—but im-

possible to go out. She hoped Romeo would
excuse her. Romeo expressed most courteous
regret at dear Meta's enforced absence; though
I, who knew him now so well, and was used
at the office to note the varying degrees of
cordiality or boredom in his reception of
authors, inferred at once from his eyes that
he was somewhat relieved at heart by dear
Meta's non-appearance. It was clear to me,
too, that Lady Donisthorpe flung Meta in-
artistically at his head; twenty times during
the evening she referred with a rigid smile
and a puff of the pouter bust to one of dear
Meta's sweet ways or to something delightful
that dear Meta had said or done for somebody. The impression she left upon me was
that Meta must be an insipid paragon, with
all the virtues and their concomitant insup-
portability. Romeo's absent smile at each
such advertisement of Meta's charming qualities—"so gentle," "so unaffected"—made
me feel convinced that he was of the same
opinion.

To put it plainly, Lady Donisthorpe showed
want of tact in her crude mode of placarding
Meta.

She had another trick of manner which
disturbed my peace of mind; like most of the

newly-enriched, she attached an excessive importance to the after all somewhat negative quality of ladylikeness. The highest praise she could accord to each achromatically charming girl of her acquaintance was that of being "a perfect lady." She flung the phrase in my teeth. Apart from the fact that it seems to imply a somewhat narrow standard, I always suspect women who insist upon this point of being themselves cotton-backed ladies.

I knew her type : she belonged to an aristocracy recruited by the names of all the best-known brands of beer, soap, and whiskey.

I protest, however, that just at first I began by treating Romeo's mother and Lady Donisthorpe with the utmost cordiality. For had I not good reasons for desiring to conciliate them ? But their treatment chilled me. I could see they had come prepared to dislike me for a conceited upstart. In return, I soon found I disliked their texture. Cornelia was cold ; I felt she regarded my humour as ill-timed. Lady Donisthorpe had the vulgar fear of vulgarity. I do not share it ; nature is vulgar enough ; we can only be "perfect ladies " on the Donisthorpe pattern by shut-

ting our eyes, shutting our ears, and shutting
our noses to most things around us. Now, I
will not shut my eyes nor my mouth either.
If facts obtrude themselves, I recognise them.
I fear Lady Donisthorpe thought it painfully
unladylike of me to have lived in the East-
End, and positively rude to tell stories of
slop-makers. She raised her tortoise-shell
glasses at the very word as a mute protest.

In fine, both were conscious of a social
barrier. So was I—with a difference. Lady
Donisthorpe moved in what calls itself "good
society," but *genteel* would have been scarce
too hard a word to describe her.

Romeo's mother swept in to dinner on Sir
Everard's arm, a three-decker under full sail.
Romeo offered me his; I gathered it was
because Meta had not arrived as expected.
Always handsome, he looked handsomer in
evening dress. A waxy white flower lay on
each plate: Romeo pinned mine on my bodice.
Lady Donisthorpe's placid eyes did not let
the action pass unnoticed.

The dinner—by which you shall understand
the food—was the best I ever tasted. The
champagne, in the judgment of one who is no
judge, was a thought too dry, but delicious.
The *mousse de jambon* was an epicure's dream.

I really enjoyed myself. Besides, I was conscious that Romeo liked my dress and felt some mild surprise to see how well I looked in it. He had hitherto known me in my black office gown alone. I forgot my poverty and was once more a lady.

It suits me better. I blossom under it. I did not even object to Sir Everard for being a millionaire; it was hardly his fault; millionaires, after all, are an outcome of the age: one can but regret that they absorb its income. Lady Donisthorpe's talk reeked of wealth till I felt it would be delightful to get home at night and see something cheap again. My seat was between Romeo and a clever young man, with keen eyes and *pince-nez*, a rising physiologist. It relieved me to learn he was not an electrical engineer; all the young men I used to meet in my præ-type-writing days had been given over to riotous electrical engineering. My neighbour's hobby was a cheerful one—the identity of genius and madness. He took *Paradise Lost* and the Vatican frescoes for premonitory symptoms of acute mania; he held the steam-engine to be a by-product of the insane temperament. Yet he urged his thesis so well that, on his own showing, I foresaw he must be qualifying for residence in an asylum. When I told him so, he cavilled at my graceful compliment. To escape his retort, I turned to the other side and joined talk with Romeo and the prebendary. I do not know what a prebendary does; his functions are more mysterious than even the archidiaconal; but I have said I love mystery; and I found the prebendary a capital talker.

Romeo was charming, as always—more charming to me that night, I fancied, than ever. Perhaps it was because he had never seen me dressed like a human being before; but also, I think, he was conscious of his mother's keen eyes and Lady Donisthorpe's steely glance; smiling ever her set smile, she felt Meta's chances were slipping from her visibly. She was an ox-eyed Hera, a little run to seed, and now almost cow-faced, but cat-like in her watchfulness. To counteract the chilling effect of the two mothers—one a feather-bed, the other a poker—and to put me at my ease, Romeo behaved with the sweetest courtesy. He talked to me; he drew me out; if I ever can be brilliant (which 'tis not for me to judge) I was brilliant that evening. I flashed to my own surprise; Romeo's admiration, and the two elder

women's scarcely concealed hostility, put me
on my mettle.

I was not angry with his mother; it was
comprehensible, of course; mothers are made
like that. We erect each other into a class,
and judge accordingly. Could any woman
with an aquiline nose, and white hair neatly
dressed by an immaculate maid, sit by unper-
turbed while her only son paid open court to
a type-writer girl? I suppose I should have
felt as she did, had I been put in her place.
Being put in my own, I naturally did my best
to let myself be seen to the greatest advantage.

So did Romeo. Having brought me there,
he was determined I should be treated with
proper respect. He insisted on talking to
me; Lady Donisthorpe's cat-like graciousness,
Cornelia's Roman austerity, only increased
his anxiety to do me honour. The more his
mother froze, the more Lady Donisthorpe,
smiling her mechanical smile, and gently
crushing, raised her tortoise-shell eye-glasses
to decide whether I was human, the more did
Romeo draw me out, and the more did I
scintillate, till at last all the table was talking
to me or listening to me. I laughed and
raised laughter; I sparkled and parried.

When Lady Donisthorpe interposed sweetly,
"And so you type-write at the office! How
fatiguing it must be!" on purpose to discon-
cert me, I had my repartee ready: "At least
it preserves me from being a perfect lady."
I could see Romeo was pleased. I was a
social success. I had justified his temerity.

In the midst of our fencing, of a sudden,
Cornelia drew out a gold pencil, wrote something on a card, and handed it across to him.
Romeo glanced at it and crumpled it up; I
could guess by his face her note had not
pleased him. "As you will," he answered
across the table; then he turned to me once
more. "That was delicious," he said; "and
what did you reply to him?"

I went on with my story. Still, I could
gather that he was annoyed; not only annoyed,
indeed, but perplexed and troubled. Dinner
solemnised, we withdrew to the comfortable
divans of the balcony for Turkish coffee. All
the party crowded round me, save the two
mammas; they did not sit apart, but, joining
our group, they preserved an austere moral
aloofness. The rest, however, redeemed their
abstention. Even Sir Everard was untrue to
poor Meta's chances. I was flushed by this
time, and the men's eyes told me I was look-

ing my prettiest. The two other girls of the
party chimed in and encouraged me. So did
the prebendary; I talked easily and brightly.
Sir Everard laughed again and again at my
sallies. He was a portly old gentleman with
a massive white waistcoat, very like a toad as
he leaned back on the ottoman. His voice,
too, was a purr; he was a toad, not a natterjack.

But Romeo had stolen away to give some
mysterious orders. I felt rather than saw
that something had gone wrong somewhere
with the machinery.

We were to adjourn to a theatre. We
drove round in state. Our stalls were near
the centre; Lady Donisthorpe in claret-
coloured velvet looked truly imposing. In
one of the interludes I looked round at the
pit. Directly behind me, in the front row,
sat a foxey-headed man staring open-eyed
towards me. It was the Grand Vizier, accompanied by a lady (no doubt "with brains ")
and concealing but imperfectly the fact that
he had been dining.

For a moment—a rare moment—I felt
really disconcerted. Under any other circumstances it would only have amused me had
the Vizier leaned forward and shouted, "Good

evening, miss," in his own dialect. But to-
night, with the eyes of those two mothers
fixed stonily on my face, I confess I trembled
lest he should rise in his seat, wave one hairy
hand, and call out loudly across the inter-
vening rows, " Allow me to introduce my fee-
on-say to you, Miss Appleton ! " I looked
away hastily, not before he had caught my
eye. I expected to see his goggle eyes fall
out and drop upon the floor : he was so
evidently surprised at my transfigured appearance. The last time he had parted from me
it was beneath the golden symbol of St.
Nicholas at the shop in the Strand ; to light
upon me there that night, dressed like a lady,
surrounded by a little court, made much of by
the men, and flushed from the Savoy, might
naturally astonish him.

However, he behaved with better taste
than I could have anticipated. He nudged
his companion, and whispered in her ear,
but kept his face averted. He was puzzled,
I felt sure ; still he had sense enough to know
that this greeting would be ill-timed, and
good feeling enough to prevent him from
forcing himself upon my notice.

When the play was over Romeo led me to
the door. I was still hot and uncertain. So

far as he was concerned this evening was for
me a great triumph ; every man and woman
there, save only the two mothers, had paid
me much attention, and, I will even venture
to add, admired me. I had looked and talked
my best, and I was satisfied with my per-
formance. But the two elder women hung
like black clouds lowering in the rear ; I
could feel them disapproving of me with
various degrees of rancour. One feared for
her son, the other for her daughter.

Very natural, I knew ; but so too was my
own attitude. No woman is born to be merely
a type-writer.

At the door Romeo led me by myself into
a well-appointed brougham. Then I knew
what had happened. Cornelia had written
across to him that she declined to take me
back in her carriage to Soho ; and Romeo, to
save me the knowledge of that slight, had
slipped away at the hotel, and ordered another
carriage to await me at the theatre. He held
my hand in his own for a brief space after he
put me into it.

"It was so good of you to come," he said.
"I have so much enjoyed this talk with you."

But the two mothers hardly gave me the
tips of their fingers, and bowed distantly

as I drove away alone, with chilly politeness.

When I got back to my room my feelings
were mixed. The jealous Gods thus alloy
our triumphs. Romeo had seen me at last as
I really was. But I had innocently disturbed
the peace of two families.

I did what every other woman would have
done in my place—sat down to a good cry
and thought about Romeo.

CHAPTER XVIII.

AN AUTUMN HOLIDAY.

I HAVE large estates in Hertfordshire and the adjoining counties, free of land tax. Some noble marquis, I am assured, lays claim to the bare loam, the ploughed fields, the turnips; but who counts mere mud? The rest is mine, to do as I will with. He may keep his rents : 'tis for me to enjoy the green lawns, the huge buttressed beech-trees, the broad circles of shade where drowsy sheep lie huddled : I own the stripling streams that break against sharp stones in the sloping stickles, or expand on the shallows between into placid pools, skimmed over by water-beetles who dart and dance nimbly in inter-lacing whirligigs. The sky overhead is mine, mine the road under foot; the scent of rain-wetted earth ; the broken song of the thrushes, the startled scream of the jay as he bursts through the rustling oak-leaves, the long sweep of the swift launching himself on

the air from the battlements of the church-
tower. All these I own, by virtue of my
freehold in the saddle of my bicycle.

Such a Sabine farm costs nought to
manage; it gives pure delight without counter-
poise of trouble. I visited mine often, both
on summer evenings and on Saturday afternoons or Sundays. Early in my time at
Romeo's a whimsical fancy seized me (being
ever irresponsible) to spend my Sabbath
mornings in such churches within easy reach
of London as were dedicated to my chosen
ally, St. Nicholas. I ran them down with
care in an Anglican Directory. If the day
were doubtful, I strayed no farther afield
than to St. Nicholas Cole Abbey, in the
City, where in a dark bay of the aisle I
prayed the prayer now nearest to my heart,
which I leave you to guess. Often as my
patron had failed me at a pinch, still oftener
had he proved kind ; I was prepared to give
him one more chance of distinguishing himself. But if the day promised to be fair,
I got under weigh betimes, and was spinning
down the roads that lead northward out
of town while the smocked milkman still
stood balanced by frothing pails in the
meadows. London lay, a vast blur, behind

me. Cows on the common chewed the cud
of penury. Their eye was pensive. Commissioner Lin showed a nasty Jack-in-office
disposition to disturb them. He was called
to heel with difficulty. Then I would seek
some country church, with low tower and
wooden lych-gate, where St. Nicholas still
bore sway, spite of iconoclast or Puritan,
to pour out my heart's wish to I know not
what Power that compels the universe.

It was my wont to lean the bicycle meanwhile against the churchyard yew or some
convenient tombstone, leaving the Commissioner in charge. He was well fitted for
the task by his unregenerate monopolist views
on private property, backed up by a fine row
of persuasive white arguments.

These weekly trips made me careless of
holiday. I waited to take my summer outing
till it should suit Romeo's convenience. I
was so much his personal secretary that
I must delay my vacation till he could take
his; and it had long been arranged that he
should put it off till late September—his
partner having desired to go away in August.

Romeo never alluded again to that evening
at the Savoy ; but I knew it had brought him
nought but disappointment. He had desired

to include me within his mother's sphere, and
Cornelia, gathering up her Roman robe, had
declined. Yet from that time he was more
deferential and more courteous, if possible,
than even his wont.

It was decided that his holiday should
begin on the fifteenth of September. As the
time drew near, Romeo grew visibly distressed
and depressed. The spring failed in his
step. I fancied he was suffering some internal conflict. His manner was distraught;
he sat at times as if he hardly heard what
was passing. It was plain to see he was
struggling within himself; irreconcilable
feelings drew him alternately in opposite
directions.

On the fourteenth he came down to the
office as usual, but sat gloomy and moody.
He did not tell us whither he was bound:
nay, more, he gave orders that no letters
should follow him. He made some mystery of his destination. At three o'clock he
went home, bidding me good-bye with more
reserve than was his wont. He kept his
glance averted. I could see he was fighting
hard to avoid breaking down. This holiday
must mean much to him. He could not look
me in the face to bid me good-bye. The

tremor of his eyelids was as of one who holds back tears with difficulty. I wished him a pleasant trip. He answered a hurried "Thank you," and rushed out to his carriage.

If I had known where he was going I think I should have followed him.

As the thought passed through my mind, Puck came in for some money out of hand. It was my duty to keep the petty cash for Romeo's personal office expenditure. "I want nine shillings, miss," the boy said; "Baedeker's 'North Italy' and Hare's 'Venice.'"

My heart gave a quick bound. I had surprised his objective. I am an erratic creature, In one second my mind was made up. I should follow him.

I had still the twelve guineas I had received for my story. Thank heaven, I am improvident. The *bourgeois* vice of thrift is one from which my family has never suffered: the Puritan blood in our veins must have been too generously diluted. Besides, have I not learned from more modern political economy that saving is the source of all the evils of capitalism?—and do I not give thanks daily that I show not the faintest tendency to develop in that direction? I have made up

my mind never to be a capitalist ; and, up to
date, I see every chance of my keeping my
resolution. So I decided to spend my twelve
guineas like a man, to please myself, leaving
Providence or St. Nicholas to make good the
deficiency. This is called faith, and is a car-
dinal virtue.

I gave Romeo two clear days' start, lest I
should travel along with him and seem to be
dogging him ; then I set out alone on my
way to Venice.

I am nothing, if not frank. Therefore I do
not seek to deny the truth that I went to
Italy on purpose to follow Romeo.

"Unwomanly!" you say. What a false
convention !

Yes, I am always frank; I think the day
has almost come for frankness. Men novelists
have depicted us as men wish us to be ; we
have meekly and obediently accepted their
portrait : to some extent, even, we have
striven, against the grain, to model ourselves
upon it. A man's ideal is the girl that
shrinks ; the sweetly unconscious girl, who
scarce knows she loves, till his strong arm
glides round her, and he clasps her to his
heart : then, with a sudden awakening, she
awakens to the truth, and knows she has

loved him long, loved him from the beginning.
That, I say, is a man's woman. Her purity,
her maidenly modesty, are quite unapproach-
able by concrete feminine humanity. She is
too delicate in mind ever to dream that she
can love spontaneously, of her own mere
motion. She loiters in the shade ; she waits
to be wooed ; she is coy, undecided, shrinking, timid.

There was a time, I suppose, when such
women were common. I do not know—for
have I not Shakespeare to the contrary ?
But the type was once true, I dare say,
and widely distributed. Still, has not time
altered it ? In the world in which we live
men are no longer ardent. We scarce affect
to conceal the fact that they grow shy of
marriage. As a necessary consequence,
women have changed too ; the woman of this
age often knows she loves, knows it poig-
nantly, breathlessly, and must use those
weapons which the world allows her if she
would gain the affection of the man who has
taken her maiden fancy. She cannot by open
means pursue him, I admit ; but she has re-
course to the immemorial feminine devices of
ruse and stratagem.

I have Shakespeare on my side, I say,

because I remember Rosalind. A man drew her; yet I see in her pure woman. She loves; she knows she loves; she longs frankly for her lover. And that is the way with women as I have found them.

Why did I follow Romeo? Why did Rosalind fly to the forest of Arden? Only once—scarcely once—had Romeo seen me as I was : that evening of the dinner. At the office, what was I but the type-writer girl? If I could meet him in Italy, he would know me as myself; we could talk more freely ; he might pluck up heart of grace to break the ice, and tell me he loved me.

For I knew he was fond of me. I could not now doubt it. When he talked to me, it was with those unmistakable sidelong glances which a woman's heart can interpret. Often he broke off suddenly. But his mother was against me ; his mother wished him to marry Lady Donisthorpe's dear Meta. In London, I knew, I had little chance to prevail over that perfect lady. But in Venice—ah, what miracles may not happen in Venice!

Mirage of the lagoons, you show men everything !

I had not set foot in the enchanted city since my father took me when I was a girl of

O

sixteen; but I remembered it well; I knew every refluent ditch of it. I could have found my way, on foot, through little aimless lanes that wander in and out, from the Piazza to the Ghetto.

If Romeo met me there by accident—if we loitered together among those churches and galleries—if I told him of my saints, if I pointed him out my best-beloved pictures, surely the struggle within him would be settled in my favour. He would prefer my wayward Gypsy-American fantasy to dear Meta's insipid graces of the perfect lady. He would know which he preferred, in spite of his mother and Lady Donisthorpe's crude advertisements.

My one regret was, that I could not take Mr. Commissioner and Elsie with me

CHAPTER XIX.

WHEN Linnæus first saw gorse in blossom he fell on his knees and thanked God. Our modern Pharisees, who say grace before meat, never, I fancy, say grace before Venice.

And yet there is only one Venice.

From the moment you arrive in the dusk at the station, and stroll down slippery steps to your gondola, to glide with stealthy movement along the lesser canals, under mysterious bridges where mysterious bystanders lean over to watch you, unknown forms that creep from dark doors in unknown streets—do you not thank God, like Linnæus, that he has brought you to Venice? And does not this feeling of gratitude and wonder for that living romance deepen on you each day that you remain? Do you not long to float for ever down those noiseless ways, to gaze up for ever at those water-stained palaces, to dream for all time among those innocent-faced St.

Ursulas ?   Mint, anise, and cumin, indeed,
when   God   has   given   us   Venice!   The
country or the south !   I pine in London.

I had loitered on my way out, breaking my
nights at Lucerne and Milan, that Romeo
might have time to reach his journey's end
with certainty before my arrival.   And on my
first morning of freedom by the motionless
lagoons, I set out early to renew my acquaintance with Venice.

I did not know where Romeo was stopping;
nor did I seek to find out.   I left everything
to St. Nicholas.   If chance should throw me
in my Romeo's way, well and good ; if chance
chose to be unkind, better so than that I
should track him.   Besides, in Venice, you
cannot long fail to meet whoever else is there.
All the world gravitates towards the centre
of the Piazza.   Sooner or later, you must
needs cross the path of everyone in the
city.

I set out from my hotel on foot ; I love
footing it in Venice ; I love the intricate
tangle of narrow paved alleys, overhung by
stone sills and rusty iron balconies, by which
the walker threads his way through the mazes
of the city.   Millionaires in gondolas never
know it.   You must ramble to see Venice.

Past little dim shops where red water-melons, sliced open, and strings of yellow carrots adorn the slabs ; past odours of salt fish and rank whiffs of garlic ; past cavernous recesses where, from murky Tintoretto-like gloom, the light of a little lamp just serves to throw up the tinsel crown of Our Lady. So suddenly at once, under the columns of a portico, into the open sky of the great square, the thronging turmoil of pigeons, the liberal flood of southern sunshine, the strong shadow of the campanile flung like a fallen obelisk on the floor of the Piazza, the mighty flagstaffs of the dead republic, and beyond them all, low and squat, a riot of white domes, the fantastic, many-pinnacled carven front of St. Mark's, glowing golden in the pellucid air of morning.

I stood still and drew a deep breath. It was even as I thought. Grace before St. Mark's: " For what we are about to receive——" There is but one Venice.

Holding my breath all the while, I drew near the great porches, with their round-arched tops, and gazed up at the mosaics. My soul steeped herself in beauty. I revelled in an orgy of jasper and porphyry. How gross to give thanks for beef and pudding, but none for Carpaccio, Bellini, Titian !

Slowly, out of the great dream of form and colour, bit by bit, as I gazed, distinct visions framed themselves — palm-leaves and lilies, robed shapes of angels, half-translucent alabaster shafts or capitals, rich foliage of acanthus, wandering lines of tracery. In the midst of it all, one little relief held my eye at last—a flat relief of quaint Romanesque workmanship, beautiful with the winning beauty of infantile art; two birds that faced one another, and pecked at a bunch of grapes—when, all at once, I was aware of a start of surprise beside me. I turned round. My heart fluttered for a second. It was Romeo.

Venice faded. Though I had come out to him, I was taken aback at his presence.

He gave a little gasp. " What, *you* here," he faltered out—" Miss Appleton—Juliet ? "

"Yes," I answered assuming an air of unconcern ; " I thirsted for a breath of Italy again. It is nearly five years since I have been out of England."

" But—this is fate !" he blurted out. " I— I came here—to avoid you."

I was in a mischievous mood. " I can go away again," I answered, looking deep into his eyes, and half curtseying. " It is not for me to interfere with my employer's holiday."

He cast me an imploring look. "Juliet," he cried, "do not jest. Do not break my heart. This is no time for pleasantry. My child, my child, I have suffered."

I saw it in his face. And yet I could not conceive what was his trouble. Could a mother count for so much? I had never known mine. "You look ill," I said; "so different from what you looked last week in London. Can I do anything for you? I—I will really go away—at once—if you desire it."

He restrained himself with an effort from seizing my hands, then and there, in the open Piazza. "*Go away?*" he cried. "*Go away?* No, *that* is not my trouble. I wish you *not* to go away. I wish you to stay with me always. Juliet, you must have guessed it; you must have known it in London. Do not tell me you did not know. You *saw* that I loved you!"

"I thought so, at times," I answered in a very low voice. "But—why then did you wish to run away from me?"

He glanced about him with uneasy eyes. "Now this has come," he burst forth, "I must fight it out boldly. I must face it like a man. Juliet, where can we go? I *must* talk —alone—with you."

"Let us take a gondola," I suggested, my heart throbbing high with joy; for I felt I had triumphed now; his mother, and dear Meta, and ox-eyed Lady Donisthorpe were wholly forgotten.

"A gondola!" he echoed. "A gondola! Ah, how clever you are! Of course! I never thought of that. There we can talk uninterrupted."

We moved towards the Molo. I hailed a gondolier. "Put up the felze," I said, "so that we may not be overlooked." The man raised the little black box, and shut us in as in a sedan-chair. Romeo gazed admiration again. "And you talk Italian!"

"Whither, signore?" the gondolier asked.

"Where shall we go?" Romeo inquired, turning to me.

"Where you will," I answered; "it is all Venice." I did not add that with him by my side all the world would be Venice.

He pointed towards the open, where we would be less observed. The gondolier nodded. Then the old fancy seized me. "To San Nicolò di Lido!" I cried. It seemed like an omen. My patron saint had always brought me luck, and his church lay before me. In this crisis of my fate I would commend myself to his favour.

I told Romeo why I chose that way. He smiled, a little sadly. "May it turn out as you wish," he exclaimed. "May St. Nicholas help us !"

I sat by his side on the soft black cushions, never uttering a word—placidly, quietly happy. I was in no hurry to speak; the sense that I had Romeo alone to myself at last was joy enough for me. He took my hand in his. I let it lie there, unresisting.

Words only spoil such first thrills of fruition. Touch is the mother-sense of love ; it needs no interpreter.

At last Romeo broke the charmed silence. I gave a little sigh as he broke it. "Oh, why so soon ?" I asked. But, like a man, he was eager to speak and explain himself. They *are* so precipitate !

"What am I to do, Juliet ?" he cried, burying his face in his hands. "Your coming has thrown me back upon my first resolve ; it has driven me from my stronghold. When I tore myself away from you in London and no longer saw your eyes—those great magnetic uncomplaining eyes of yours, those eyes that have bewitched me—I made up my mind that I

must go through with it now, and try to forget you. Not try, but pretend ; for it would
be all pretence. Since the first day you
came, daily and daily you have meant
more and more to me. It was hard to
break away from you, but I broke away
and came here, so that I might be free from
the spell ; for while I saw your eyes I could
think of nothing else ; and now chance has
thrown you in my path again, and—I cannot
go through with it."

" Not chance," I murmured low ; "not
chance—but St. Nicholas ! I have come with
the money that my story brought me."

He smiled at my little conceit, for I had
told him in London of my half-fanciful cult of
the poor maids' saint, and I had called my
little tale "A Ward of St. Nicholas."

" You are a brownie ! " he cried, gazing at
me. " You wild thing, what brought you
here ? "

I laughed. " The Gotthard railway—and
my love of adventure. I was sickening of
England ; I had a migratory instinct, like birds
when they gather on the telegraph wires in
autumn, or restless Spanish sheep in spring,
when they herd and leap, uneasy to be driven
to their pastures in the mountains."

"What a wild thing you are!" he repeated. "A brownie, a brownie! I wonder where you got it from?"

"From my gypsy ancestry, I suppose," I answered.

"Gypsy—but I thought you told me you were American?"

"On my father's side, yes; but on my mother's Lowland Scot or Anglo-Indian. She was a Baillie of the Borders; and I suspect all borderers of sharing the blood of the Faas and the Petulengros. There was plenty of intermarriage."

"No doubt," he mused. "The difference must have been slight between a moss-trooper and a gypsy. Each had much the same gentility. And, indeed, I remember the 'Lord and Earl of Little Egypt' was summoned to Edinburgh as a peer of parliament."

"At any rate," I said gaily, "whether 'tis true or false, it accounts, to my mind, for the Meg Merrilies vein in me. I was born a random vagrant in the world, a peripatetic philosopher. I love movement, I love free-dom—Bohemia. Why, I could tell your fortune now if you cared to cross my hand with silver."

He gazed into my eyes. "I do not doubt

it," he answered, "for it lies in your hands
to-day."

I thrilled and was still. The gondola
glided over the glassy water.

Soon he began again. "Gypsy, I want
your help. You must *make* my fortune, not
tell it. Show me how to act. Show me how
to get free. What can I do in this crisis,
Juliet—my Juliet ? "

"How can I answer ?" I replied. "'Tis for
your own heart to say. I know you are fond
of me. But—your mother has money, I suppose, and you prefer your mother."

He withdrew the arm that lay half round
me, and sat up facing me in surprise. "My
mother ! " he cried. "My mother ! Why,
Juliet, my child, what do you mean ? It is
not my mother I think of—not her, but poor
Meta ! "

A pang darted through me. "Then you love
her !" I exclaimed ; "that woman's daughter !"

"Love her ? I do not say that. Yet,
Juliet, consider ; put yourself in her place :
I have been five years engaged to her ! "

It burst upon me like a thunderbolt. Why
had I never guessed it ? From the first day
we met I had taken it for granted—unreservedly, unthinkingly—that Romeo was

heart-free and unfettered as I was. Even
when I met Lady Donisthorpe I imagined too
fast that she was flinging Meta openly at his
head, but not that he was betrothed to her.
My own heart must have blinded me. Now
that I realised it all, I stood aghast at the
way woman's instinct had failed me. How
had I managed to misunderstand? I saw in
a flash that the conflict I had observed in
Romeo before he left London was a conflict
in his soul between love and honour.

He seized my hand again. "It is *that* that
made it so difficult," he whispered. "From
the first day *you* came I began to love you.
I fought against it hard, oh! so hard; I tried
to talk little with you. Day after day I
felt you sitting there, with your great gypsy
eyes fixed ever steadily on your sheet of
paper, and your heart going forth to me. I
knew it went forth to me. I could feel it in
the room. A subtle wave or thrill throbbed
ever between us. I began to love you; and
still I fought hard. But the more we talked
together the more did I feel you were the
woman God made for me, and that Meta was
not. At last I had a great struggle—a great
struggle with my heart, and came out of it as
I thought victorious. I fled from you here,

where the Donisthorpes had come, to remain with Meta till the day I married her. It was what honour demanded ; I made love yield to honour."

I withdrew my hand slowly. " Give me time to think this out. It has burst upon me so suddenly. Oh, Romeo, till this moment I never dreamt you were engaged to her."

" Why *Romeo ?* "

I smiled, though my heart was aching. I remembered that he did not know what I had always called him. Now I told him my fancy. " You have never been anything but *Romeo* to me," I murmured.

He seized my hand again. "Juliet, I *am* your Romeo. I felt it from the first. We were meant for one another."

"I know it!" I cried. "I know it! And this woman, who is not yours, has stolen you from me. You are mine by natural fitness ; and she took you, *she* took you ! "

We leaned back on the seats and mused. The gondolier sang low to himself a soft Venetian love-song.

After some minutes I began again. " Of course," I murmured, "it is Lady Donisthorpe's daughter."

"Of course. Five years ago I proposed to her."

"Then *why* did you not marry?" I cried vehemently. "I *hate* these long engagements! They are vile for everybody!"

"Her stepfather would not permit it till she came of age. She is a ward in Chancery, and he has influence with the court. Till her marriage her mother has some interest in the property, and Sir Everard, to preserve it, being fabulously rich already, made an excuse that a publisher was hardly the person to whom she might expect to aspire—though he permitted, or rather encouraged the engagement."

"And she is not yet of age?"

"In October."

I gave an impatient wave of the hand. "But she was a child when you proposed to her!"

"A child? We were both children. We did not know our own minds. The Nemesis of it is that I know mine now, while she remains still at the childish standpoint."

"She loves you?"

"In her baby way—yes; else it were all easy. But it would break her poor heart. Such a trusting little creature!"

" And *you* love *her?* "

" Juliet, I thought I did once.   But then, I had not learnt what love meant.   She was only my Rosaline.   I did not know the world of difference between a sweet little wax doll, with masses of light yellow tow for hair, and a woman, a thinking woman, with heart, soul, brain, courage—a woman who could face life full of intrepid self-reliance ; a woman with nerve, audacity, spirit; a woman with Homeric love of danger and adventure ; a woman made dearer by her sense of humour, the merry twinkle of her eye, her gay laugh at misfortune.   I feel now that I need a comrade and a help, meet for me.   Someone who could brace me up for the battle of life ; someone with great thoughts, fine fibre, noble impulses.   I cannot go back to Meta.   I could have done it last night.   This morning, with you by my side, I feel it, I know it, impossible."

He drew a long breath.   I lay back on the cushion.   " Romeo," I said, pleading my rival's cause, " you *must* go back to her."

" Never ! " he answered, " never ! "

I temporised.   " This is not a question to decide all at one.   Let us think it over slowly; let us lay it—before St. Nicholas ! "

" If I lay it before St. Nicholas," he cried, " with you beside me, the oracle can give but one answer, I warrant. For I want you; I need you ; my whole being cries out for you."

We paused again. The water was cat's-eye green. The inexorable gondola glided on towards the Lido.

We talked it over clause by clause. A light began to break upon me. The nearer I drew to San Nicolò the clearer grew the light. Ought a man to wreck two lives—his own and the girl's whom he means to marry (for my private fate I ignored)—in order to satisfy a false sense of honour? What, after all, was this honour? A bugbear dressed up to frighten us from the truth. And what was the truth ? That Romeo was rushing madly into marriage with a girl for whom he was not fit, and who was not fit for him.

" Romeo," I said at last, "could you make her happy ? "

" That's the rub," he answered. " It could hardly be for long. I could give her my hand, but not my heart ; for my heart, my heart, Juliet, is yours—yours only."

" Then for *her* sake set her free," I cried.

P

"The whole man—body, soul, and spirit—or nothing."

"So I think," he murmured. " The question is, when one has made a mistake, a mistake that involves final ruin for two lives, which is the better, after all: to repair it beforehand, while repair is still possible, or bow to an antiquated ideal of honour, an ideal that comes to us from an age when women were toys, all alike, and run one's head into a noose from which there will be no escaping? For her sake, as well as my own and yours, ought I not to tell her, frankly but gently, that this marriage she desires must mean misery for both of us?"

I tried to be impartial, though impartiality is hard when your own love and life lie trembling in the balance. "You ought," I answered, " if you feel sure you cannot truly love her."

"Juliet, I can never love anyone but you. I know you for my counterpart. My love did not come suddenly; it grew up by degrees from living so near you; and it has grown, grown, grown, like a vast growth in my heart, till it has absorbed my nature. I have watched you every day, talked with you, listened to you. You know me and you understand me. But Meta, dear little soul, she seems to me like a child. I cannot share life with her. I can only take care of her. You have originality, initiative; Meta's soul has the shape that her mother has put upon it. Look how you loved and appreciated my verses! Your criticism, your help, were of infinite use to me. In each word that you altered I felt you were right. Your suggestion of 'harmonious' in that last line where I had written 'consistent' made a full close for the sonnet, in sonorous organ music, and turned my prose into poetry. Whereas, when I gave Meta my book she read it through, and then kissed me. 'How clever of you, you dear boy, to be able to write verses!' Would *such* a help be meet for me?"

I clung to his hand; it was hard to decide; but in a very low voice I faltered out, "I think not, Romeo."

He talked of my poor attempts at writing stories; he praised them, as he had always done. "You will be famous yet, my child; and I shall be proud, whatever comes, that I was the first to encourage you." He appreciated me, I appreciated him; surely, if marriages are made in heaven, we two were moulded for one another. Not alike, but com-

P 2

plementary. And then, how rash to dream
of marrying one woman when, even before
marriage, you love another better! Is *that*
the way to insure a happy home? Is that the
safe path to a life of wedded confidence?

We drew near to San Nicolò at last. "Let
us go in," I said seriously, "and submit ourselves to the saint. His body lies within.
We will kneel together before it."

"But I thought you told me St. Nicholas
lay throned in a gorgeous shrine at Bari?" he
objected.

"Why, of course," I answered. "What is
the use of being a saint if you cannot have
two bodies, and be in two places at once?
And what is the use of faith if it does not
enable you to believe the impossible?"

"I *do* believe it," he answered; "since I
came to Venice to be out of your enchant-
ment, and found you here, more deliciously
enchanting than ever. The fascination of
your eyes——."

I cut him short with a gesture; but I was
glad he praised them.

We landed by the steps, and entered the
sailors' church. I led Romeo up to a scal-
loped niche by the tribune, where I had often
prayed as a girl with my father. We knelt

down, side by side, before the jewelled shrine
that contains the blessed dust of St. Nicholas
of Myra, I hope not irreverently. I may be
what the Warden at our Guild was fond of
calling me, "an amiable heathen," but at least
I am sincere. Tears stole down my cheek.
I asked with an earnest heart for light, for
guidance. We know not, indeed, whose
saintly bones repose at peace within that
sculptured marble altar-tomb; nor does it
matter to me much whether they be or be not
those of the benign bishop of Myra. I accepted them as the symbol of that Power,
above ourselves, to which our hearts go forth
at moments of doubt, of fear, of anguish; and
to such a Power I prayed unfeignedly, that at
this turning-point of my life I might be led
aright, might form the just judgment, un-
biassed by self-profit, holding an equal scale
between myself and my rival.

As I knelt there a single flashing ray of
light beat down through a little window above
upon San Nicolò's altar-slab. It gilt the
niche for a moment; it fell in gold on the tes-
sellated floor; then it passed away as a cloud
covered the sun. Rightly or wrongly, I accepted the omen. Tears stood in my eyes
still, but they were tears of gladness. "St.

Nicholas has answered," I whispered. "What did he say to you, Romeo?"

Romeo looked me in the face solemnly as he made reply. "He said, 'Better tell her early than tell her too late. Save her while she can be saved, and let three hearts be lightened.'"

Venice hung like a haze. The row back to the Molo was a lane in Paradise.

CHAPTER XX.

"WHEREFORE ART THOU ROMEO?"

AT the Molo we parted. The Donisthorpes,
Romeo said, must long have been expecting
him, fidgeting that he did not arrive; he
knew not what lame excuse he could rake up
to satisfy them. It was agreed on both sides,
however, and impressed with last words, that
he must not break poor Meta's heart prema-
turely, by too abrupt an avowal of his new
decision. We were to break it by degrees—
to give her three days of purgatory. Meanwhile, Romeo promised he would not see
me again, at least to speak together; though
he asked leave, wistfully, to pass under my
window once each morning and smile at me,
just so as to make sure of my presence. I
wanted this interval; I wished to see whether
he would remain firm to his purpose when he
was removed for a day or two from that
"magnetism" of my eyes on which he dwelt
so strongly.

I spent the three days of grace in wandering about Venice. For the most part, I
avoided the great square, St. Mark's, the
Academy—all the familiar tourist haunts—
because I did not desire collision with the
Donisthorpes. Most of my time I devoted
to the out-of-the-way streets and the out-
of-the-way sights, which are so infinitely
amusing; the funny little alleys where
the true Venetians stroll; the funny little
campi, where old men and children lie
stretched in the shade on the north side
of some small church, as fallow-deer huddle
on the north side of the domed oaks in a park
at noontide. Every turn revealed some passing picture. As I had said to Romeo, it was
all Venice. Not a remote sunless lane, with
walls of peeling plaster, tufted with pellitory,
that is not dear to my heart ; not a sluggish
side canal, into whose stagnant green water
branches of acacia and trailing sprays of Vir-
ginia creeper hang from beyond the moulder-
ing garden grill, but I love and cherish it.
Little Romanesque windows, high up on some
red-washed steeple, with twin round arches,
tall and narrow, held apart in the midst by
one twisted column ; great patches of sunlight
falling through quater-foils in dazzling relief

on the deep recessed gloom of the loggia;
wee bridges that rise, arched like a cat's back,
over streams strewn with cabbage-leaves,
where market boats from Mestre, laden high
with pumpkins, crawl slowly down the channel
—do I not know them all? Are they not
etched on my brain by some fadeless process
of mental photography?

In spite of my haunting these remoter by-
ways, however, I did once by accident catch
sight of the Donisthorpes. They were seated
with the prebendary at a *café* in the great
Piazza, as I crossed it one afternoon on my
way home from San Zaccaria, where I had
been feasting on saints in the placid enjoyment of every form of martyrdom. Sir
Everard, leaning back on his chair and sip-
ping black coffee, with a small brown cap
pushed well off his forehead, a brown tourist
suit, and a capacious yellow waistcoat, amply
displayed in front of him, looked more absurdly like a fat toad than ever. Lady
Donisthorpe, smiling sweetly upon Venice
in general, with her ladylike softness, her
mechanical amiability, her pouter-pigeon
suavity, yet showed marks about the eyes of
some inner dissatisfaction. They did not observe me; I stole close behind them, anxious

to see the immaculate colourless Meta; I wished to know for myself what manner of girl she might be; but she was not with them—gone off, no doubt, for a stroll round the square with Romeo. That thought drove me quickly home; like a frightened rabbit, I rushed under the clock-tower and along the thronged Merceria to my hotel on a side canal; I could not have endured to see them together like lovers.

Had I no qualms meanwhile? Aye, marry, had I? Do you think I slept much through those three long nights of suspense and torture? If I tramped from church to church and picture to picture during the day, 'twas but to escape from my own stinging thoughts for a moment. I argued it all out over and over again with myself. When we two had been seated side by side in the gondola—Romeo's arm half stealing round my waist, my head half pillowed one second on Romeo's shoulder—the question of ethics had been translucent as crystal. We saw quite clearly our course was mapped out for us by eternal equities. Even in Meta's interest, I was advising him for the best. "The whole man," I had said—"body, soul, and spirit—or else nothing!" That was woman's full

gospel of the new dispensation. Less than
that could be no true marriage. And "is it
not better, under such conditions, to change
one's mind early than to change it too late?
Is it not better for you to speak the truth,
even at great risk of pain and humiliation to a
woman you have loved, than to tie her for
life to a man who cannot give her his whole
heart unreservedly, enthusiastically? Is it
not better for her to be made miserable once
than to be made miserable for ever?" In
advising Romeo to break off this one-sided
engagement, was I not advising him most of
all in Meta Donisthorpe's interest?

At times I even felt as if I had succeeded in doing a great favour, unasked, to
Meta.

But in the dead hour of night, when all
Venice slept, and the last "Stalì!" had
answered the last "Premè!" under my bedroom window, one stanza of "In Memoriam"
kept ever recurring most inopportunely to my
mind; I heard it in the creaking of the vane
on the Dogana, in the lap of the water against
the honeycombed walls, in the sigh of the
wind through the arches of the belfry. It
was a reproachful sound—the voice of that
conscience which I flattered myself the

generation of whom I am one had analysed away for ever.

> " Hold thou the good ; define it well ;
>   For fear divine Philosophy
>   Should push beyond her mark, and be
> Procuress to the Lords of Hell."

The Lords of Hell ! The Lords of Hell ! It clanged with the hour from the great Campanile ! Was that where my sophisms were taking me, I wondered ? The Lords of Hell ! The Lords of Hell ! Had I advised Romeo aright, as the woman who loves a man should strive to advise him at dangerous passes ?

On the third day of the three I rose early from my sleepless bed—tired of tossing off the quilt—and wandered out by myself eastward through the tortuous labyrinth of elbow-bending streets that spreads between St. Mark's and St. George of the Slavonians. I was bound no whither in particular ; I let each narrow flagged alley, each canal-side causeway, lead me onward where it would ; but, without design on my part, I found myself at last on the small paved platform with the slimy green steps that catches the morning sun, in front of San Giorgio degli Schiavoni. "San Giorgio !" I thought to myself ; "I must stray in here for a while for rest and

meditation. After Nicholas of Myra, has not
the ever-blessed George been most of all my
patron ? Let me lay before him my doubts—
a poor maider' doubts ; it may be that the
courteous young saint will resolve them."

I pushed aside the padded curtain, and sat
down on one of the seats. Venetian women
were there with their babies, praying—dark-
haired, dusky-eyed, poorly-clad, eager-spirited.
For a while my eyes strayed to those ever-
exquisite Carpaccios, high ranged on the left-
hand wall, which tell the pretty tale of the
tutelary saint with naïve Venetian idealistic
realism. I scarce knew which of the two chief
actors I admired the more—in the episode of
the slaying of the dragon, so familiar to me
from my own life, the beautiful, graceful youth,
with his loose golden hair rippling free on the
wind ; or, in the scene of the baptism, the
kneeling Princess Cleodolind, her long, fair
tresses flowing richly down her back as she
bends to receive the sacrament of the font at the
hands of her chivalrous and devout deliverer.
St. George, I fancied, in his earnest, clear
face, somehow recalled my Romeo ; but the
Princess—I shuddered : what ill-omen was
this ? The Princess whom he baptised was a
fair-haired maiden. I knew Meta was fair—

had he not spoken of her "masses of yellow tow"? A cold thrill ran down my spine. Oh, St. Nicholas—oh, St. George, avert the omen!

I pulled out my little silver crucifix, and, clasping it tight, decided to lay my case before the Madonna herself, who reigns in the altar-piece. Am I a Catholic, then? you ask. That is alien to this story. There are three subjects which I decline to discuss: bi-metallism, the sex question, and my religious convictions.

As I bent my knee before Our Lady on the shrine a low sob by my side distracted my at-tention. It came from a young girl a little apart in the gloom. Her face lay hidden in her hands—small gloved hands, like a lady's; but her fine-fibred hair was golden and luxuri-antly abundant. I glanced from her to the Carpaccio, and from the Carpaccio to her. Yes, it could not be gainsaid—this was the Princess Cleodolind.

Had her St. George proved untrue? She was crying bitterly.

I knew at once that was the right explana-tion. The sound of her sobs betrayed it. For there are species in crying. There is the cry of the mother for the loss of her son;

there is the cry of the wife for the faith-
lessness of her husband ; there is the
cry of the maiden for the defection of
her lover. Each has its own note, recog-
nisable at the first sound to those who have
once heard it. We talk in such cases of
woman's intuition ; it were truer, I think, to
call it inference, for inference it is from
delicate observation. All women observe
keenly the symptoms of emotion; at moments
of exaltation or passion they observe them
with an almost miraculous acuteness. I knew
in a second that Cleodolind had lost her lover's
heart; and I guessed in a flash that Cleodolind was Meta.

She was dressed like a lady ; and out at
this early hour ; when she and I, alone of our
class, driven from our beds by alternative
aspects of the self-same problem, were abroad
among the fisherwomen.

I gazed at her with the respect one always
accords to sorrow. My heart misgave me.
How easy it was in the gondola to philoso-
phise in the abstract ; but here, on dry land,
and in sight of this poor child with the breaking heart—philosophy in the concrete seemed
to present its own fresh difficulties.

Of a sudden she raised her face, and glanced

across at me, piteously.   Her eyes met mine.
I started.   The wisp of a figure, the pathetic
blue eyes, the sunny fluff of hair: it was
Michaela.

I took it in with a great gulp.   Michaela
was Meta, then, and Meta Michaela.

I could not understand it, for the inscription
on her card said, not Donisthorpe, but "Miss
Allardyce"; and had she not told me that her
Christian name was Margaret?   But I had
no time to think it out just then.   With a
little cry of pleasure, she came over to me,
still weeping.

"You dear thing!" she whispered, holding
out her gloved hand, "what a comfort to see
you!   I want to have a talk with you.   You
were so good to me at Holmwood."

I saw it was inevitable.   I must face Meta
now.   I took her hand in mine, with a deep
sense of repentant treachery.   "Come out
with me, dear," I said, for she melted my
heart.   "Tell me all your trouble."

She pressed my hand in return.   "I knew
you would be good to me," she answered.
"You are odd, but oh, so good.   I saw it in
your big eyes the first day I met you.   Do
you know, your eyes are magnetic; they seem
to draw one."

"So I have been told," I answered bitterly.

"Where can we go to talk?" she asked. She had a caressing voice. "I am sure you will do me good. And I do so want to talk this over with somebody else besides mamma. Mamma is like a feather-bed. She is kind in her way, but so soft and comfortable. Nothing seems to make a dint in her."

Inventiveness forsook me. I had no suggestion to offer except another gondola. And even at that moment, when the world whirled round madly with myself for pivot, I was dimly conscious, as one is often conscious of such trifles at a great crisis, that always in Venice, when people wanted a *tête-à-tête*, they must have taken a gondola. Nowhere else in that tangle of narrow streets and small squares could one go unobserved for a second.

We called a gondolier. "Where shall we tell him to take us?" Michaela asked. It was not in her nature to suggest a route spontaneously.

"Out on the open," I replied. "We shall be less overlooked there." Then I added a little morosely, "If you are not afraid I shall drown you."

She smiled through her tears. "You were always so queer," she said, "but so kind."

Q

She did not guess how much more reason I had now for drowning her. She jumped lightly into the boat; she was a light little atomy; you could have blown her away with a good puff, like thistledown.

The gondolier took us across by San Giorgio Maggiore. Michaela sat by my side, holding my hand in hers. If ever in my life, I felt guilty that minute.

So all those months I had been doing in earnest what I had said in jest—unconsciously playing Carmen to her Michaela. I had stolen away her Don José—and had never known it!

She told me hurriedly how the man to whom she was engaged had always seemed to love her, oh, so much—till five months ago; how, since that time, his love had been gradually fading; how it had faded all away, till she was wretched, hopeless!

She cried so intensely that I laid her head on my shoulder. 'Twas a soft little head. I felt like a man to her as I tried to comfort her.

"Five years," she sobbed out: "five years—all forgotten!"

"You must have been a child at the time when you began to love him," I murmured.

She raised her head. "Yes, a child.
That's what makes it so much worse! We
have loved and been loved since we were
both children. Every thought, every pleasure, we have shared with one another. I
was cycling with him that day when I first
met you. We have grown up together. He
has grown into my heart—ever closer and
closer."

"What is his name?" I asked, trembling.

She told me. I hardly needed to ask
it.

"Why, I know him a little," I said.
"But I thought—he was engaged to a
daughter of Lady Donisthorpe's."

"Yes, of course. Lady Donisthorpe is my
mother."

"But—her name is Meta; and you are
Margaret Allardyce?"

"Mamma married again; I told you I had
a stepfather."

She went on with her story. She loved
him more and more. Her heart was bound
up with him. After so long a time, too! If
he had told her three years ago—— But
five years—you could never make five years
seem nothing.

"And can you account for it?" I inquired,

to see how much she knew, stroking her sunny hair with my hand as I did so.

"You *dear* thing! How sweetly sympathetic you are! Oh, yes, but it is almost too dreadful to tell. A hateful woman—a typewriter girl at his office! Could you ever have believed a person like *that* would come between us?"

"Perhaps," I ventured to suggest, "she did not mean it."

"Did not mean it? Oh, she did: the dreadful creature, she has bewitched him! He loves *her* best now. And yet, you would think that the years must count; the years must count!" She sobbed, and became inaudible.

"Has he told you of her?" I faltered.

"Oh! no; he says nothing. He only lets me feel it. But mamma met her once at a dinner Toto gave at the Savoy—a hateful vulgar creature! Mamma and his mother both spoke to him of the way he treated her—the attention he paid her—bringing a woman like that to dine with ladies, it was unpardonable."

"Some type-writers *are* ladies, Michaela," I put in softly. "I am a type-writer myself."

"Ah! yes, but that is different! you are so

sweet, so gentle. You know so much; you have been brought up like a lady; you have sympathy and magnetism. This other creature—mother said it was horrid to be in the some room with her. So loud, so noisy! And she's here now, she's here; she has followed him to Venice on purpose to thwart us. He came out to stay with me till the day we were to be married. And this woman, when she saw her hold on him was failing, rushed after him to prevent it. Can you believe such wickedness? Mamma saw her with him in a gondola. Oh! I can't bear to say it, dear, in a gondola, near the Riva, with his arm around her!"

"Perhaps," I hazarded, "when she came here she did not know he was engaged. Perhaps, if we could speak to her we might play upon some chord in her better nature."

Michaela looked up at me admiringly. "You beautiful, broad-minded person," she cried; "how good you are, how tolerant! You make allowances and excuses for everyone, I declare! How I wish I was like you! But she *has* no better nature, I believe. Mamma says she is a person lost to all sense of shame. Why, the stories she told at that dinner of Toto's about the places she had been in and

the people she had met were quite beyond,
you know, quite beyond; oh, too dreadful for
anything."

I risked another card. "My dear little
friend," I said, "I speak of the thing that I
know: she *has* a better nature." (Oh, God, how
it was battling now against love of Romeo in
her heart; how it was grappling and struggling!) "I am almost sure I have met this
girl of whom you speak. There is a type-
writer stopping at the same hotel as myself,
and I think she was out in a gondola the other
day with your Romeo —let us call him Romeo;
it is 'more real and agreeable,' as Dick Swi-
veller said to the Marchioness, and 'tis the
only way in which I can talk about people."
I maundered on, to gain time, for though
outwardly I was jesting, within I was fighting wild beasts at Ephesus. "Now, she has
talked to me of your Romeo, and I assure
you solemnly, when she arrived in Venice she
had not an idea he was engaged—of that I am
confident."

"Ah, but she knows it now, I am sure;
and yet, she bewitches him!"

I played one card still, a more doubtful
and dangerous card than any. "Perhaps," I
answered. "But the years must count. You

are right in that. Remember, as you say, I
am (I hope) broad-minded. I try to see
things from everybody's point of view. From
yours, I see now that Romeo is behaving—
cruelly. From the type-writer girl's, I see
that she loves him deeply, very deeply ; but
'tis a new love, fresh grown ; however firmly
it may have rooted itself, it has no claim on
the score of age as against yours ; and if she
is told so calmly and frankly, she may perhaps realise it. From Romeo's, I see—well,
more than I like to tell you." I paused and
hesitated. The effort to gain time made me
didactic. "Life is the interaction of indi-
vidualities," I said, "each seeing things its
own way. Justice is the attempt to reconcile
them. Let us try here if we can make this
type-writer girl see something a little beyond
her own point of view—see, as you say, that
the years must count. She is not wholly bad,
whatever Lady Donisthorpe may tell you. I
will be your ambassador. I will speak to
her ; I will speak to Romeo. I will try to
make them feel what you have made me feel
—that the years should count. And I will
come to San Giorgio of the Slavonians to
tell you what success I have had in my embassy at this time to-morrow."

She brightened up at the idea. She thanked me profusely, "He loves me still," she said, "a little; only, this girl bewitches him. Oh, I have read about her eyes and her hair in his verses. He thought no one knew; he put it so darkly—all wrapped up in words; but I could see they were hers, though he thinks me so silly. I am clever enough where one's heart is concerned; I can catch at a straw then. But if *she* were once away, I am sure he would come back to me." She nestled into my shoulder. "You *dear* thing!" she cried again, grinding her teeth with affection, "you have put fresh hope in me."

"Thank you, dear," I answered. "Do you remember at Holmwood I called you Michaela, because you were so fair, like the girl in the opera? Now, this type-writer girl is dark, and she has be. 1 playing Carmen to you—stealing your love away from you by her clever ways and her blandishments. She has gypsy attractiveness. But, Michaela, I am sure she did not mean it. If she had known of you, if she might have seen you, she could not have wronged you. Do you recollect what I said to you in the train that day—' You dear little thing, no one could ever

hurt you!'? Well, I am sure the type-
writer woman would feel as I do—if she knew
you. But I want to make you promise me
one thing—if I bring you back your Romeo,
you will forgive her?—you will never again
call her a horrid creature?"

She soothed my hand in turn. "I could
promise you anything," she said. "I never
knew anyone so tender and helpful."

We bid the gondolier turn. She held my
hand still; blue sky in her eyes shone after
the rain. "Only to think," she cried, "I
have met you three times—no more; and
yet I feel you are a dear friend—the sort
of friend who would do anything for one."

"You have reason," I answered.

We returned to the Molo. A crushed heart
and a doubtful one had embarked in that gondola; a crushed heart and a doubtful one
disembarked from it again. But they had
changed places.

Three days ago I had seen through the
gates of Paradise. To-day an angel with a
flaming sword stood to bar my entrance.
And, worst of all, I knew his name was
Justice.

CHAPTER XXI.

ENVOY PLENIPOTENTIARY.

I TRAILED back to my hotel, surely the most abject soul in Venice. Michaela's misapprehension of my motives I did not resent; the American eagle in my breast had scarce a flap left—a more draggle-plumed bird I had seldom seen. But all was at an end. I had lost my Romeo.

My interview with the first of the two delinquents whom I had engaged to lure back to the path of rectitude I got over quickly on my way home. It was not a hard one. The culprit, sitting meekly on the penitent's bench, listened to all my blame with a contrite heart ; and in consideration of her contrition I condoned her evil deeds. It was easy to condone, for here I knew all, and to know all is to forgive all. Michaela would have forgiven had she seen into that poor mangled heart as I did.

Looking back over my life dispassionately

from the calm height of twenty-three, as if I were looking at some other woman's life, I think I can say I have never acted wrong—grossly and unforgivably wrong—given the circumstances. It is those alone that others fail to understand. If they understood, they must sympathise where now they blame us.

Could Michaela have watched, stage by stage, the slow organic growth of my love for Romeo; could she have felt the inevitability, the consecutiveness of the way it unfolded; could she have realised its foregone certainty as an outcome of two natures, I think, dear little soul, even she would have hesitated to call me " that horrid woman."

But it was all past now, and she had regained her Romeo.

One culprit had recanted. I had still to face my embassy to the second high contracting party.

I sat by the balconied open window of my bedroom and looked down into the canal. It was almost the hour for Romeo's daily passage. Slow barges with firewood drifted lazily by, then a boat-load of purple egg-fruit and heaped golden melons, with a gondola or two loitering on the look-out for passengers, like our London crawlers.

At last my heart began to beat, not high as it had beaten the two previous mornings, but with a low foreboding. Another gondola swung with a graceful curve round the huge bosses of the corner palace ; in it, a familiar crush Tyrolese hat, and beneath the hat, Romeo.

He gazed up at me, smiled, and waved one hand ; but his look was anxious.

I leaned out and called to him : " Romeo, Romeo, Romeo ! "

He rose and glanced at me with checked breath and eager eyes.

" Come up here," I faltered ; " I want to speak with you."

" In your room ? " he cried, hesitating.

I felt it was no moment to stand on false convention. " Yes, in my room," I answered. " Have I not told you I have confidence in myself and my guardian angel ? "

He waved the gondolier to the steps, leaped lightly out, English athlete that he was, and was with me in a moment.

I might have treated the situation melodramatically and hissed out at him " Traitor ! " (But then, it is true, I unconsciously shared his treachery.) Instead of that I treated it like a woman, and burst into tears before him.

He drew a chair by my side. His white face quivered. "You have seen Meta?" he faltered out.

I could feel his heart throb.

"Yes," I answered, "I have seen her, and —I find I know her. Romeo, we were all wrong. We were deceiving our own hearts with specious sophisms. She said to me in her soft small voice, all choked with tears, 'The years must count; the years must count!'—and—she was right when she said it!"

He flung himself upon me. "Juliet!" he cried, "dear Juliet, I too have suffered. I have battled with my own soul. The beast has fought the angel and the angel the man in me. When I see her, when I am with her—so gentle, so childish, so cruelly hurt by my coldness, or what she thinks my coldness— how can I have the heart to break to her the resolution we formed? Yet the moment I leave her I know it is the right one. It would be wrong of me to marry her now, having found my true mate—wrong for her own sake. 'The whole man—body, soul, and spirit—or nothing.' Do not go back on your own words. It would be treason to the eternal cause of woman."

He spoke so vehemently that I faltered.

Then Michaela's pale face, with the gentle blue eyes swollen red from weeping, came up like a mist before me. "You shall not wrong that child!" I cried. "Much as I love you, Romeo, not even for my sake will I allow you to wrong her. She is right and we are wrong; the years must count. She has grown up with your love inextricably twined by rootlets and tendrils through the fibre of her being; to tear it away now were to tear her very heart out. She lives on your affection. To see is to understand; before I saw her I thought as we thought at the Lido. Now I know better. I will not allow you to wrong her."

He drew away a step and looked me over with his keen eyes from head to foot. I quailed before his glance, so full it was of admiration. "My Juliet!" he cried. "Why talk? I love you for *this* better than I have ever loved you! That you can contemplate such a sacrifice for honour's sake and for justice—the greater to the less, you to Meta —shows me you are more worthy to be loved than even I thought you. I *cannot* marry any-one but you. You, you, you! O, God," he flung himself upon me in an ecstasy, "to

think that in a world which holds such a
woman as you they should call upon me to
content myself with that wax doll of a Meta!"

I untwined his arms quietly. I was fighting
now the battle of my sex, and I almost forgot
myself in my advocacy of Michaela. "You
shall not speak so of her!" I cried; "the girl
whom you have loved for years—the girl to
whom you have uttered such vows, on whom
you have bestowed such kisses. It is an
insult to our sex. The years must count—
the years and the endearments."

He stood away and began again. "Juliet,"
he murmured, in caressing tones, and in his
flute-like voice, as if he loved to repeat my
name, "there is one woman in the world
supremely fitted for me. She has courage,
she has wit, imagination, fancy. She can
hold her own; vivacious, brave, strenuous.
One of her stray black elf-locks is worth all
Meta's loose gold. Yet she has high purpose
enough to plead another woman's cause
against her own heart, her own happiness.
Her brain is alert; her eye electric; her soul
womanly. The more she argues, the more
does she make me admire her, reverence her,
worship her. Go on pleading if you will, dear
heart; I love to hear you, to watch you; but

every word you say, every hand you move,
for Meta, only strengthens my resolve that
you I will have, or I will have nobody.
Against your will, I will make you happy."

He sat down by my side again, and bent
towards me coaxingly. In his low sweet
voice he began to reason. I listened while
he said over again every argument we had
used together by the shrine of St. Nicholas,
with others like them. If he married Meta,
how could she hold his heart? She would
be the mistress of his house, a sort of superior
pet bird, to be tricked out in fine feathers, to
be coaxed, stroked, fondled ; but not a wife.
If he married me, we should go through the
world together, equally paired, soul-wedded,
each mirroring the other's mind, each respecting, admiring, reinforcing the other. We
two were natural complements. Why seek
to throw him back from the higher upon the
lower ?

I listened and trembled. What he said
was so flattering to one's own inner vanity,
seemed so exactly what one thought in private when one dared to be frank with oneself,
had such a show of eternal and immutable
reason, that the temptation to go back on my
word and accept his argument as true was

almost irresistible. If I had not seen Michaela, I think I should have yielded. Love, one's own heart, the man one adores at one's feet, these are dangerous assailants. But I closed my eyes, and there Michaela's blue eyes rose up, appealing to me in the gondola, with that piteous cry, "The years must count; the years must count!" wailed out ever from her heart; and I knew I was fighting the common battle of womanhood. If I were to turn traitor now, I should turn traitor to whatever I had within me best worth calling a conviction.

He seized my hand and kissed it. When the lips of the man you love touch you, it is hard to refuse. But I drew the hand away. He followed it up. His breath was warm upon my cheek. My bosom rose in a tumult. I began to fear I had presumed too much upon my guardian angel. If Romeo pressed me hard now, I must throw Michaela overboard—I must forget his honour, the years that count, the battle of my sex, all that is sacred on earth, everything save myself and Romeo. If he asked me, I must say, "Yes; let the white girl go; I will be yours, my Romeo."

Then, conscious of my own weakness—

R

with an impulse as if from without, of a
sudden I flung myself on my knees, and
prayed silently and earnestly for strength to
do right, strength to refrain from betraying
Michaela.

Romeo stood off with clasped hands, observing me in dead silence.

I rose from my knees another woman. The
soul of womanhood found voice within me.
"Romeo, dear Romeo," I cried, facing him,
and speaking like one inspired, "it is not a
question for you; it is a question for me. I
love you with all my soul; but I refuse to
marry you. I will not be a traitor ; the years
must count : go back to Meta !"

He caught my hand in his. I let it lie like
a stone. "Do not send me away," he implored. "Let me stop with you a little !"

I sank into a chair. He did the same. "But
remember," I gasped, between two sighs,
"this is final."

Tears rose to his eyes. He began to speak
once more. "You must not think, dearest,"
he said, "I have not felt for Meta. Not all
these nights have I slept; but, honestly, in
the dark, I thought it out, and I came to the
conclusion it would be best in the end—even
for Meta."

"Romeo," I said, raising my eyes, "do you love me?"

He made a hasty gesture as if he would fling himself upon me once more.

I waved him off with one open palm. "Then promise me, promise me, you will go back to Meta."

"I cannot!" he cried. "I love you."

"Will you go back to Meta?"

It was a hard, long struggle. We parried, thrust, marched, countermarched, evaded; but I had taken it in hand, and I determined to finish it. Inch by inch falling back, but still fighting, he gave way. He saw I was in earnest. Behind each line of defence, each logical hedge, he tried to argue it out again. I cut him short with a hasty gesture. "A man, yes, he can forget the years; but a woman— never!"

At last, worn out, he promised. In the agony of my excitement I took his yielding as a personal triumph. I had asked of my lover a difficult gift, and by dint of woman's armoury, had prevailed on him to grant it.

"But—you will stop on at the office?" he asked at last, holding his breath.

I turned on him. "How could I? For

R 2

Meta's sake, impossible ; for my own, an infamy."

"And—I must never see you again ? "

I bowed my head. "These things are made so. It is *yes* or *no*. If *yes*, for life ; if *no*, then never."

He advanced towards me, with his lips trembling visibly. " I may say good-bye ? " he faltered.

My heart leaped to break its strings. I knew not what to say. At last—" Yes, if it is good-bye, and if you go back to Meta."

He seized me in his arms. I will not deny that for one whole minute I lay there sobbing, happy. It is little, for a lifetime. Then I moved him away softly. He clung to me, panting. "Now you must go," I whispered. ' Do not tell her it was *I*. Keep my secret!"

I opened the door. For a second he lingered. I waved him away. I could endure it no longer. Looking back and breathing hard, he passed through into the passage. I turned the key in the lock to satisfy myself that that embassy was fulfilled ; then I fell on the bed, and cried a low cry, " Romeo ! Romeo ! "

CHAPTER XXII.

I CLING TO THE RIGGING.

So my poor little Odyssey had come to an end in shipwreck! Mr. Samuel Butler must be wrong, after all. I doubt a woman's ability to handle these sustained epics. I was to get no farther on my way to Ithaca than the episode of Phæacia. Nor would any Nausicaa come forth to aid me.

After I had cried my heart's full—cried till that point when you begin to leave off and to laugh like a child at nothing, for pure weariness—the humorous element, which inevitably enters into all human tragedy, pressed itself upon me. On the stage, art never lets these incongruous incidents intervene at critical moments to disturb the current : in real life, they *will* obtrude their faces, like Paul Pry ; and 'tis my misfortune and my good luck that, with some grain of Heine in my composition, I cannot shut my eyes to them. So here, the comic muse, masquerading as Common

Sense, stepped in with one grotesque reminder:
" You have no money to pay your way back
to London."

Now, gypsy or American or Anglo-Indian
or what you will, I am true Briton in this,
that whatever misfortune lowers, I see one
path of safety—the road home to London.
" If only I could get back to London ! " is the
Briton's heart-felt cry of distress in a foreign
land. He can starve in comfort, so he may
starve in Piccadilly.

I have already explained that I am wholly
free from the vile vice of prudence. To take
no thought for the morrow is to me an article
of religion, though 'tis rare among those who
profess to accept it as a divine injunction.
Acting on this principle, I had bought a single
second-class ticket to Venice, as my funds
were insufficient to pay for a return. It was
my idea, when I started, to trust for my
journey home to the saint who lies at the Lido.
Now, however, I found myself in an awkward
predicament. St. Nicholas had played me a
last bad turn. I had bought perforce a new
travelling costume before I left England, for
I recognised that my rational dress with the
knickerbockers would harmonise ill with the
genius of Venice ; the rest of my cash in

hand had gone for beds at Lucerne or Milan, and passing necessaries. I stood face to face with an Italian court of bankruptcy ; liabilities, my hotel bill ; assets, five paper lire.

To borrow from Romeo was now clearly impossible. And the canals are so redolent of thirty generations of Venetian refuse that suicide does not offer here its normal allurements.

This brought the revulsion. I lay on my bed and laughed to think that, broken heart or not, I could not get away from Venice.

By evening, I had a headache. I was crying once more. But the worst of headache is that it never kills.

Early next morning I woke from a short snatch of sleep with a dull pain in my left side. It was moral, not physical. I rose, to ease it by action. *Oubliez ; voyagez !* I had still qualms of conscience—I who fancied I had dissected conscience out of existence : but this time they were reversed. Had I done right, after all, in speeding Romeo to his fate ? Would Michaela be a mate for him ? Was it not better as it was before—for the greatest happiness of the greatest number at least ? St. Nicholas, help ! John Stuart Mill, stand by me !

I dressed, bathed my red eyes, and went out to keep my appointment. I was early at San Giorgio, but Michaela was before me. As I lifted the heavy curtain, her eyes shone happiness. In her radiant countenance I read my doom. She was calmly, serenely joyous. I beckoned her to the *campo*. She flitted out, and with a charming baby impulse flung her arms around me.

Tears rose in my eyes. It was sweet to see her happy. I held her hand and said nothing.

"Well, he has explained all," she whispered. "You were a dear to speak to him."

" Explained ! " I cried. How true it is that explanations explain nothing !

"Yes, he told mamma he did not know the type-writer girl was coming to Venice. He went out with her in a gondola because he met her by accident—and it was such a surprise to him; and he wanted to avoid mamma. But he is not going to see her again, and I believe he will dismiss her."

"No, dear," I said gently, unable to restrain myself, "he will *not* dismiss her, because— she will go away of her own accord. She does not intend to remain with him. I have seen her, and I can assure you she is better than you think. She did not know Romeo was engaged ; and when she fully realised it she relinquished all claim to him, or rather admitted she had never had one. Michaela, dear child, you must not be hard upon her. You promised to forgive her. I feel sure she has suffered, for she loved him devotedly."

"How good you are!" Michaela cried. "You sympathise so with everyone!"

"She has promised me," I went on, "that she will never again see him, that she will avoid him with care, that she will not speak to him nor write to him. She will try to forget him, though to forget him is as impossible for her as for you. But she will be true to you ; she will keep her word. I can answer for her as I could answer for myself; she spoke with such earnestness. She is tearing out her heart; but because she thinks it right she will tear it out ruthlessly."

Michaela smiled a tranquil smile. "And it is all right now," she said. "We are to be married in October, as we arranged originally."

We walked along the canal. We walked side by side, but great gulfs separated us. At last I spoke again. "You forgive her, Michaela?"

"Oh! yes, dear, I forgive her. If she did

not know, of course it was natural. He *is*
such a dear! She could not help falling in
love with him!"

"So I feel," I said. She glanced up at me
with inquiring blue eyes. I think for a
second she half suspected the truth, for I had
spoken too deeply.

We walked on in silence a little farther.
Then Michaela began again, brimming over
with her happiness. "I haven't a quarter
thanked you. But I *am* so grateful! You
were a sweet to see them both. You will
come to my wedding?"

"No, dearest," I answered, driving back the
tears with a fierce effort. "If so, I should
be breaking a solemn promise."

Again she seemed to suspect, and again the
doubt went from her.

"It was all a mistake," she continued, in a
childish, sunny way, "a passing cloud. And
Toto seemed so distressed, I couldn't help feeling sorry to see him so sorry for me. It has
touched him very deep. He cried a great deal.
He has been crying all the time. But it is all
right now. We shall be quite happy!"

I swallowed a lump. What a child it was!
And *there* lay the irony. I think I could have
spared Romeo better had I felt I was sparing

him to more of a woman. Self-sacrifice for
some great soul would be easy: but for a bit
of thistle-down! And yet I loved her.

"I told mamma how kind you had been,"
Michaela went on, quite guilelessly, "and she
wants to see you so much. You must come and
dine with us at our hotel. How long do you
stop in Venice?"

I paused and reflected. I had done her a
service—a very great service; what need to
stand on trifles? For I do not share the
vulgar dread of putting myself under an
obligation.

"Dear little Michaela," I said, spanning her
arm with one hand—it was so fairy-like and
tiny—and drawing her towards me, "I will
confess the truth. I am travelling with that
type-writer girl. I know her intimately.
Now, I want to spirit her away from Venice
at once, so that she may not see Romeo, and
that Romeo may not see her. It would be
awkward for both of them. But I have no
money. I borrowed from you once and repaid you faithfully; if I borrow from you
again I will repay in like manner. This is a
worse strait than Holmwood. I shall need
six or seven pounds. My dear, can you lend
it to me?"

She drew out the dainty purse. " Why, of course, dear, if I have it. Fifty, a hundred and fifty, two hundred lire ; will that be enough for you ? "

" Yes, my child," I gasped out, taking the crumpled notes and crushing them in my folded hand. " If I work my fingers to the bone you shall have it back."

We walked on towards the Molo. O grey, grey Venice ! The greatest happiness of the greatest number. Back, back, Stuart Mill ! Get thee behind me, Satan ! A gondola approached. I hailed it.

" Where are you going ? " she cried, surprised.

" Away," I said, " at once. It is better— safer ! I will give the devil no chances." Then to the gondolier, " Hold off a little ! "

He held off beyond jumping distance. Michaela hung over on the bridge close by, wondering.

" Michaela," I cried, " now I will tell you ! " An impulse came over me; I could no longer resist it. " It was *I* who stole your Romeo's heart by mistake ! It was *I* who played Carmen and beguiled your Don José. It was *I* who sent him back. *I* am the type-writer girl ! "

"You!" she cried, waving to me to return. "Oh, you dear thing, come back! If it was you, how good you have been! Why, I can see it in your face. You have suffered for my sake! Come back, and let me kiss you!"

"No, dearest," I said, melting. "I must go. I dare not trust myself. Good-bye for ever! Good-bye to you; good-bye to Romeo. Give him that message for me; I will never again see him." I turned to the gondolier. "Quick, row for all you are worth! To my hotel first, then on to the railway station!"

If this book succeeds I mean to repay Michaela. Meanwhile, in any case, I am saving up daily every farthing to repay her. For I am still a type-writer girl—at another office.

THE END.